FULL TILT

ALSO BY NEAL SHUSTERMAN

NOVELS
Bruiser
Challenger Deep
Chasing Forgiveness
The Dark Side of Nowhere
Dissidents
Downsiders
The Eyes of Kid Midas
The Shadow Club
The Shadow Club Rising
Speeding Bullet

THE ACCELERATI SERIES
(with Eric Elfman)
Tesla's Attic
Edison's Alley

THE ANTSY BONANO SERIES
The Schwa Was Here
Antsy Does Time
Ship Out of Luck

THE UNWIND DYSTOLOGY
Unwind
UnWholly
UnSouled
UnDivided
UnStrung
(an e-book original)

THE SKINJACKER TRILOGY
Everlost
Everwild
Everfound

THE STAR SHARDS CHRONICLES
Scorpion Shards
Thief of Souls
Shattered Sky

THE DARK FUSION SERIES
Dreadlocks
Red Rider's Hood
Duckling Ugly

STORY COLLECTIONS
Darkness Creeping
Kid Heroes
MindQuakes
MindStorms
MindTwisters
MindBenders

Visit the author at storyman.com and Facebook.com/NealShusterman

FULL TILT

Neal Shusterman

SIMON & SCHUSTER BFYR

NEW YORK LONDON TORONTO SYDNEY NEW DELHI

ACKNOWLEDGMENTS

A roller coaster is only as good as its support, and this one would not have been possible without an infrastructure of exceptional people. Thanks to Danny Greenberg and Ginee Seo for believing in *Full Tilt* from the very beginning. Thanks to my assistant Sharon McKeag for work beyond the call of duty. Thanks to my parents for always being there with love and wisdom. And thanks to Patricia, Maureen, Michelle, Jean, and all the fictionaires, who have crossed the line from friends to family.

SIMON & SCHUSTER BFYR

An imprint of Simon & Schuster Children's Publishing Division
1230 Avenue of the Americas, New York, New York 10020

For information about special discounts for bulk purchases, please contact Simon & Schuster Special Sales at 1-866-506-1949 or business@simonandschuster.com. The Simon & Schuster Speakers Bureau can bring authors to your live event. For more information or to book an event, contact the Simon & Schuster Speakers Bureau at 1-866-248-3049 or visit our website at www.simonspeakers.com.
Also available in Simon & Schuster Books for Young Readers hardcover edition.
Book design by Daniel Roode
The text for this book is set in Aldine.
Manufactured in the United States of America
This Simon & Schuster Books for Young Readers paperback edition November 2009
12 14 16 18 20 19 17 15 13 11
The Library of Congress has cataloged the hardcover edition as follows:
Shusterman, Neal.
Full Tilt/Shusterman, Neal.—1st ed.
p. cm.
Summary: When sixteen-year-old Blake goes to a mysterious, by-invitation-only carnival he somehow knows that it could save his comatose brother, but soon learns that much more is at stake if he fails to meet the challenge presented there by the beautiful Cassandra.
ISBN 978-0-689-80374-1(hc)
[1.Carnivals—Fiction. 2. Brothers—Fiction. 3. Self-perception—Fiction. 4. Near-death experiences—Fiction. 5. Horror stories.] 1. Title.
PZ7.S55987Fu 2003
[Fic]—dc21
2002013867
ISBN 978-1-4169-9748-1 (pbk)
ISBN 978-1-4391-1525-1 (eBook)

For Brendan, Jarrod, Joelle, and Erin, who always remind me how much fun the ride is!

1

"I Go Places Sometimes"

It began the night we died on the Kamikaze.

I should have known the night was jinxed when Quinn lost his hat on the Raptor. I wasn't sure where on the roller coaster he lost it because I didn't ride with him; my friends, Russ and Maggie, did. I had volunteered to wait in line for Icewater Rapids.

"What a nice guy," Maggie had said, giving me a peck on the cheek. Well, nice guy or not, I had my own reasons.

The loss of Quinn's hat was the first trauma of the evening, but not the first of Quinn's life. Whole galaxies of traumas revolved around my brother. I knew he wouldn't part with his hat easily; it was one of his prized possessions—a black baseball cap with a very distinctive design on its face. Not the insignia of a sports team or a designer logo—that wouldn't do for Quinn. No, his hat featured a rude cartoon of a hand with its middle finger up. He loved that hat because he could flip everyone off on a continual basis.

He was still grumbling about his loss as he, Maggie,

and Russ joined me in the line for Icewater Rapids.

"There should be catch-nets beneath the ride," Quinn complained. "They're gonna pay. Russ should have caught it—he was behind me!" As if the whole world were to blame.

"Ignore him and maybe he'll go away," Russ said, waving his beefy arm dismissively. Russ is what you might call a disenfranchised jock. He muscles up regularly, lifting weights, but never lasts more than a month in any of the sports he's tried, because he loses interest too quickly. Maybe that's because so many of the other guys on teams just try to impress the girls, while Russ had no need: He and Maggie had been dating since the beginning of recorded time, with no end in sight.

As for Maggie, she couldn't have cared less about Quinn's ravings. She checked herself out in a tall mirror—one of several distractions placed in the long line to break up the monotony. "Tell me the truth, do I look fat to you?" she asked me.

"You're kidding, right?"

"No, seriously."

Russ just laughed.

"Maggie, it's a fun-house mirror. Of course you look fat. That's the point."

She sighed. "I know that, but fun-house mirrors never usually make me look *this* fat."

"Scootch down a bit," Russ said, "and you'll be fat in all the right places."

She poked him in the stomach for that one. Warped mirrors aside, Maggie was slim and nice looking. Smart, too. But to hear her talk, you'd think she was dumb and ugly, always comparing herself to the other girls in school.

"Congratulations," I told her, glancing once more at the mirror. "I always said you've got a distorted view of yourself. Now you really do."

She threw me a twisted grin, and Russ, thinking the grin was meant for him, clamped his muscular arm around Maggie's waist. I sometimes wondered if Maggie got bruises from the way Russ held her—like, if he let go, she might get away.

You're probably wondering how I fit into this little high school equation. Well, I suppose if the others are variables, I'm the constant. Constantly studying, constantly busy, constantly shuttling from swim team to debate team to home with the regularity of a celestial clock.

"That's what I like about you," Russ once told me. "You've got a level head—and I don't mean just the haircut."

As far as the equation went, I'd be out of it soon, on account of the way I tested out of high school. Not that I'm a genius or anything. I'm just a mix of a little bit of brains, a whole lot of studying, and a knack for multiple-choice tests. Blend that with a single parent earning minimum wage, and you get a scholarship to New York's Columbia University at sixteen. I was scheduled to leave next month, right after summer vacation, skipping my senior year of high school entirely.

"Columbia?" Russ had said. "Wow, I didn't even know you spoke Spanish!"

Maggie had told me he was kidding, but we both knew he wasn't. Let's face it, if my bulb was halogen, Russ had an energy saver. But that's okay. He had other things going for him. Like his easygoing personality. Like Maggie.

Me, I was between girlfriends. So when we took our little road trip to Six Flags, instead of a date, I ended up with Quinn.

I turned around, noticing that Quinn had stopped grumbling about his hat. That's because he was gone.

"Forget about him," Russ said. "He'll turn up eventually, and even if he doesn't, no great loss."

I shook my head. "If he gets into trouble, we'll all get ejected from the park." Which happened once before, when Quinn took an M-80 and blew up an animatronic mime.

"You know that's what he wants," Maggie said, "to make us all look for him."

"He's a waste of life," said Russ, and it annoyed me. *I* was the only one allowed to call Quinn a waste of life.

"Next time bring a metal detector," Maggie suggested. "Easiest way to find him."

I laughed at that. She was, of course, referring to Quinn's many facial accessories. Studs, rings, and dangling things. They weren't just in his ears, but in his eyebrows and nose. He had one in his lip, too. Call me old-fashioned, but I figure a thirteen-year-old like Quinn could get away with one, maybe two rings before maxing out the face-to-metal ratio.

I asked Russ and Maggie to wait for me when they

were done with the raft ride. Then I wound my way out of the line until I came to a wide pathway that was almost as crowded as the line. In an amusement park this big, I knew if I let him get too far away, I'd never find him. And Maggie was right; he'd like that just fine. He'd ruin my night by making me worry where he was and what kind of crazy thing he was doing, then he'd show up at the car an hour after closing, with a smug grin stretched across his ring-filled face.

Fine, let him get lost, I told myself. *I don't care.* But the problem was, I did care, and that annoyed me even more.

For a long time everyone thought Quinn was autistic. Hard to believe that, looking at him now. Now he was just a self-centered royal pain. But when he was a baby, he would turn all his attention inward, never making eye contact with anyone. He was almost three and a half before he even spoke. It happened right before our parents split up. We went to one of those cheesy carnivals that came to town every year. Dad took us on a kiddie coaster. Quinn smiled—and back then Quinn never smiled. Then, when the little ride grinded to a halt, Quinn spoke.

"Daddy, more."

We were speechless. Until then Quinn had never put a coherent thought together. It was as if the ride had stimulated something in my brother that had always been dormant. Dad moved out a few weeks later. It was on the night of our annual viewing of *The Wizard of Oz,* just about the time that Almira Gulch turns into the

Wicked Witch of the West. I still can't watch that movie without getting a sick feeling in my stomach, like it's my own house spinning inside of a tornado.

Our father probably would have left a few years earlier had Quinn not been born. Quinn wasn't planned. He was an "accident." Enough of an accident to keep Dad around until Quinn was three. Since he left, our lives have been a roller coaster of Mom's raging romances with men who weren't good to her, or to us.

As for Quinn, that first ride opened the door to bigger things. Stimulation and saturation. His life was a festival of excess that could not be contained. Deafening music, eye-popping bright colors, sugar added to almost everything he ate. Quinn's life was a bullet in a barrel ready to explode.

I searched the amusement park for fifteen minutes before I found him. I would have found him sooner had I been thinking like a lunatic, to whom breaking laws is a lifestyle choice.

About a dozen people stood in the middle of a wide pathway, looking up at something. I followed their gaze to some imbecile climbing the support scaffolding of a roller coaster. He was at least fifty feet high and leaned dangerously toward a piece of cloth wedged between two crossbeams. It was a hat. That's when I realized that the imbecile and I came from the same gene pool. And the law my brother was trying to break now was the law of gravity.

"Is that part of the Spider-Man show, Mommy?" I heard a little kid next to me ask. I hurried toward the roller coaster, ready to kill my brother, if he didn't do the job himself.

"Have I ever told you what a psycho you are?"

I stood on the exit stairs of the Raptor, looking out at Quinn, who clung to the support beam about six feet away from me. I looked around to see if any guards had noticed him out there, but for the moment Quinn's antics had found a security blind spot.

"Hey, *defib*, okay? I had to get my hat." He stretched his hand out toward it, but it was still just out of his reach.

"Did you ever consider engaging your brain?" I easily grabbed the hat from where I stood on the exit stairs.

He sneered at me, but he did seem a bit red in the face. "Oh, sure, do things the easy way." There was something else about him too. Not now, but when I'd first arrived. I'd seen the way he'd reached for his hat, as if he weren't hanging fifty feet above the asphalt. As if he didn't notice where he was until I'd brought it to his attention. There were times that he sort of slipped out of phase with reality—a holdover, I guess, from those early years when he was so locked in his own private universe. It wasn't just that he didn't see the big picture. Sometimes he saw a different picture entirely.

Now Quinn looked down, taking stock of his situation, and shrugged, swinging to another girder closer to the stairs, still using the ride's infrastructure as his own personal jungle gym.

"Isn't it enough that you drive Mom crazy?" I asked

him. "Is it such a stretch for you to be normal just this once?"

He tossed his head, flinging a lock of his uneven hair out of his face. "If that's what you are, I'd rather be deviant."

Unable to reach the railing of the stairs from where he hung, he grabbed a bar above his head and let his legs swing free, as if the fifty-foot drop beneath him were nothing. A sizable crowd had gathered below, gawking and pointing.

That's when I noticed the vibration. I felt it in the staircase railing before I heard or saw it: a shuddering of metal crashing downhill. It came to me in an instant what I already knew but had forgotten until that moment.

The Raptor was a hanging roller coaster. The bars Quinn dangled from were part of the track.

Quinn realized it too, and he tried to swing himself closer to the railing but didn't have enough momentum.

All at once the train swung around an outside curve, its riders screaming with joy, completely unaware of my idiot brother directly in their path.

I leaned out as far as I could, grabbed Quinn by the waist, and wrenched him from the hanging track. I almost lost him, but I got enough of him over the rail to flip him onto the stairs. We tumbled on the steps, while just past the railing, the Raptor sliced past, a blur of green and black, gone in an instant.

I should have been relieved, but saving Quinn was such a regular pastime for me, all I could feel was anger.

"I'm tired of saving your friggin' butt," I told him, although *friggin'* and *butt* weren't exactly the words I used.

Then his eyes glazed over for a second.

"I go places sometimes," he told me, his voice as thready and distant as his eyes. "Don't know why I go places . . . I just do."

It caught me off guard. He was around six the last time he said that. It was a whisper at bedtime, like a confession. A secret, too fragile for the light of day. *I go places sometimes.*

But right then I wasn't feeling too sensitive. "Next time you go, bring me back a shirt." He snapped out of whatever state he was in, and something inside him closed up like a camera shutter. He glanced defiantly at the ride that had almost turned him into roadkill, then looked back to me.

"Nice save, bro." Then he put on his hat, effectively flipping me off without lifting a finger.

2

An Invitation to Ride

We found Russ and Maggie standing dangerously close to the entrance of another roller coaster—the new one, hyped up to be the mother of all thrill rides. Flaming fragments of Japanese Zero planes decorated the entrance. The ride was called, of course, the Kamikaze. The thing was a mutated hybrid, offering the bone-jarring rattles of an old-fashioned wooden coaster along with the loops and corkscrews of a high-tech steel one.

I refused to look up at the dizzying monster above me, but I did see the twisting nightmare of a line in front of us, which ended at the sign saying SIXTY MINUTE WAIT FROM THIS POINT.

"Icewater Rapids was totally geriatric," Russ said. "Blue hair and denture cream all the way."

"I doubt we'll get to ride the Kamikaze if we don't get in line now," Maggie said.

Russ levered his arm around her in his usual rib-crunching style. "It's now or never."

I gave him a look of casual annoyance. "Look at that

line. What a waste of time. Let's find something else to do."

Quinn rolled his eyes, adjusted his hat, but said nothing.

"Are you kidding?" said Russ. "Miss the main attraction?"

"Do you really want to wait for an hour in that line?"

"The ride's only been open a week, and I hear they already have three lawsuits," Russ said. "You expect me to miss a ride like *that*?"

It was a good point, and I knew the three of them would end up riding. I also knew if I kept debating, one of them would suggest that I go do something else. I wanted that suggestion to come from them, not from me.

Just then some pimple-faced, buzzard-necked employee removed the chain that blocked the ride's second line—a line that was completely empty.

"No way!" said Quinn, so excited that he almost drooled.

Suddenly I had no reasonable argument not to ride.

My panic built as people ran to the empty line like passengers leaping from the *Titanic*. "Guys, what's the big deal, anyway?"

Maggie took a dangerously deep look at me. "Are you scared, Blake? Don't be—you'll have fun."

"Scared? Don't be ridiculous," I told them. "I love roller coasters."

"Yeah, sure," Quinn said with a sneer.

I threw Quinn a warning glare. He swore he wouldn't tell anyone—but then what did Quinn's word ever mean?

"Blake's terrified of roller coasters," Quinn said.

I tugged on the sputnik hanging in his ear, and his head tilted to one side. "Ow!"

Russ looked at me like I was someone he didn't know. "He's kidding, right?"

I stammered a bit. Lying is not one of my better skills.

"Blake hates airplanes and roller coasters and fast cars," Quinn said.

"That's not true!"

"It is and you know it!" Quinn turned back to my friends. "He's a grade-A chicken. Yellow as a school bus!"

That's what did it. I don't know if Quinn realized what he had said. I didn't even think he knew about the School Bus Incident. But whether it was intentional or not, it got my feet moving.

"Sure, I'll ride. Can't wait." I tried to sound casual about it, and that's hard to do through clenched teeth. I forced myself forward, keeping my pace steady as I wove through the empty line. I didn't slow down until I saw the big warning sign in bright red letters. You know the one: YOU MAY NOT RIDE THIS ATTRACTION IF YOU ARE PREGNANT, HAVE BACK TROUBLE, A HEART CONDITION, HEMORRHOIDS, WATER ON THE KNEE, BLAH-BLAH-BLAH. I slowed down, glanced at the emergency exit, and got an unwanted blast of déjà vu. I knew I hadn't been here before, but the feeling wouldn't go away.

"What's the matter?" Russ asked. "Feeling a pregnancy coming on?"

I laughed, but I had a hard time tearing my eyes away from the emergency exit sign. Quinn, on the other hand, never even looked. Like everything else in his life, he crashed forward, caution the first casualty.

It took only a few minutes to reach the ride. Quinn, of course, grabbed the front car, smiling back at me. "Next stop, Willoughby," he said, quoting the old *Twilight Zone* episode. "Room for one more."

Russ and Maggie took the seat behind him. I stood there, frozen.

"C'mon, Blake," Russ said. "One last thrill before the ivy."

Ivy, I recalled, is what they generally put on a grave.

"Very funny," I said a moment before I realized that he really meant Columbia University, which is an Ivy League school. Duh. I took my place next to Quinn, my feet uncomfortably crossed in front of me. I pulled down the lap bar, double-checked it, then triple-checked it. Quinn snickered at the expression that must have filled my face.

"Are we having fun yet?"

"Just shut up, okay?"

The little train jerked forward and began to ratchet up a steep climb toward the first drop. "You gotta live for this, bro," Quinn said. "Live for it, like I do."

The Kamikaze dragged us heavenward and reached the peak of its first drop. We lingered for a moment at the peak, then hurled into a suicide plunge. My stomach tried to escape though my eyeballs. My brain became a pancake pressed to the dome of my skull. Quinn whooped and wailed, loving the feeling. *You gotta live for it,* he had said, but right now I just wanted to live *through* it.

The safety bar offered no safety at all, and all at once I was back there again. . . .

Seven years old, spinning out of control. My first ride . . .

No! I told myself. No, I would not go there. I wouldn't think about it. I pushed the memory down so deep, not even the Kamikaze could shake it loose.

The roller coaster bottomed out and turned sharply to the left, spinning into a double corkscrew. Quinn's hands were in the air as he screamed with the thrill of the ride. I gripped the safety bar, gritting my rattling teeth.

The Kamikaze doubled back, and the force of the turn cut into my side as we shot toward an insane loop. My head was pressed forward by g-forces. The earth and sky switched places, and back again. Then, as we came out of the loop, I caught sight of a wooden support strut tearing away from the weblike scaffolding of the Kamikaze. The thick pole plunged like a felled tree.

"No!" I screamed. *"No!"*

It wasn't my imagination. It was real! Crossbeams fell away next to me. The rattle of the ride intensified. When I turned my head, I caught sight of the damaged part of the ride, but we were speeding away from it, hitting a trough and rising again. Then the ride took a wide U-turn and headed back toward the damaged section.

Another support beam broke away. Big heavy white timbers tumbled down, bouncing off the track, taking more of the ride with it. Others saw the danger now.

"Do you see that?" yelled Quinn. *"Do you see it!"* The screams of fear were the same as the screams of joy. I tugged at my lap bar, but what did I think I could do? Jump?

The damage was right in front of us now. The last falling crossbeam pulled away all the support beneath the track, leaving us to face a rickety trestle. Just the track and nothing beneath. For a moment I thought we'd make it across, but the left rail fell away and then the right, leaving a twenty-foot gap and a hundred-foot fall.

I could do nothing but scream as the Kamikaze left the track, the rumbling and rattling giving way to a deadly silence as smooth as wet ice, then a vertical drop, spiraling at the full force of gravity. My face was an open wail. The wind, the light of the park, the whole world disappeared into my screaming mouth as the bottom dropped out of the world, turning into a black misty pit.

Darkness.

More darkness . . .

And then the lights of the Kamikaze station blazed around me as the little train came to a jarring stop and the lap bars all popped up in unison. The ride was over, and I was left with the mind-frying memory of something that could not have happened, but did.

"Cool!" screamed Quinn. "Did you see how the track fell away?"

"Yeah," said Maggie. "It looked so real."

"I wonder how they do that," Russ said.

I looked up. The support struts and dangling cross-beams rose against gravity, reassembling themselves like the collapsing bridge at Universal Studios. Only then did I see the single hidden track that brought us into the vertical dive and back into the station once the false track fell away.

The ride attendant turned to me. "Hey, you have to get out. If you want another ride, you'll have to get back in line."

I gladly vacated my spot.

On the way out we were all given pins that said I DIED ON THE KAMIKAZE.

My hand shook as I tried to drink a Coke. I wished my friends weren't watching me.

"Didn't mean to scare you, dude," Russ said. "I thought everyone knew what was going to happen. Jeez, they've been showing the commercial for months, before the ride even opened."

Maggie put her hand on mine. "It's okay. To be honest, I was pretty shaken up myself."

I went a little red at Maggie's touch. Russ noticed how Maggie held my hand, and he put her in his lover's choke-hold. "He'll get over it," Russ said.

We were on the midway now. Quinn was hurling baseballs at a stack of resistant silver bottles that just wouldn't fall from the pedestal. He wore his Kamikaze pin like a Congressional Medal of Honor.

"Why don't you stick it through your belly button?" I suggested.

He pointed at his hat and threw another ball. "That ride was a life-altering experience," he said, although his life didn't seem altered much at all. Even now, he hurled those balls at the bottles with a certain fury—the same fury that followed all of his dealings. His high from the ride was already fading, and I knew he'd be impossible to live with once it was entirely gone.

Up above, a new batch of victims plunged from the fracturing beams of the Kamikaze. I forced myself to watch, this time seeing the single dark track beneath the falling train. It crashed out of sight, the ground rumbled with the force of an aftershock, and a voice I didn't know spoke to me.

"You like the fast rides?"

I turned to see a girl watching me as I watched the ride. She was the one running the ball-toss booth. *A life-altering experience.* Quinn's words came back to me, but I couldn't say why.

"I . . . uh . . . what?" This girl was beautiful. Beautiful in a way that even now is hard to explain. Like an impressionist painting in a soft gallery spotlight.

"I asked if you like the fast rides."

"I . . . can't get them out of my mind," I told her, which wasn't entirely untrue. She smiled as if she knew exactly what I meant. Her hair was long and red—the kind that must have been brushed a thousand times to make it flow in a perfect fall of copper silk. And there was something about her eyes—blue as glacier ice, yet hot as a gas flame—reflecting the chasing lights of the midway. They seemed like windows to some other place. They also seemed familiar.

"There are better rides than these," she said, in as close to a whisper as the loud park would allow. She was older than me. Eighteen at least.

Like all the girls will be, I thought. *They'll all be older than you when you get to college next month.* Looking at her was like looking into my future.

"I'm Cassandra," she said with a smile.

Is she flirting with me? It was a heady feeling. I got a knot in my gut, like I was still on the Kamikaze, turning a tight loop. No hidden safety track here.

"I'm Blake." I held out my hand to shake, and she put a ball into it instead.

"Try your luck," she said. "This one's on the house."

By now Russ and Maggie had taken notice of the way Cassandra was looking at me and the way I looked back. Russ smirked knowingly. Maggie's mood took a turn toward sour. "Why are we wasting our time here? Let's ride something," she said.

Quinn was getting angrier with each ball he threw and each dollar he lost. "These stupid games are all rigged." He stepped away, and I took his place.

A life-altering experience.

I shook off the strange feeling that I would have recognized as a premonition if I had had any sense whatsoever. Then I took aim and hurled the ball at the little pyramid of bottles, hitting them squarely in the center. Those bottles flew like they were hit by a freight train, not a baseball. Looking back, I think those bottles would still have fallen even if I had hurled the ball at the moon.

Quinn jolted in disgust. "Oh, man!"

"We have a winner," said Cassandra. She reached above her to a menagerie of stuffed animals and pulled one down. She didn't give me a choice—*she* decided which one I got. The roller coaster rumbled again, and the air filled with the screams of its riders.

"Enjoy," she said as she handed me my prize.

It was a bear, but this bear was one sorry specimen. Its head was lopsided, its bright red eyes were too small and too far apart, making it appear both angry and congenitally stupid at the same time. Its fur was an uneasy shade of greenish brown, like what you get when you mix all of your paints together.

"That bear is as inbred as they come," said Russ.

The bear wore a bright yellow jersey bearing the number 7. *School bus yellow*, I thought, but I shook the thought away. On the jersey was a large pocket in the center of the bear's chest. The edge of something stuck out of the pocket.

I reached in and pulled it out. It was a white card about the size of an index card. On it was a strange symbol in bright red:

"What's that supposed to be?" Quinn asked.

I flipped the card over to see what was written on the back.

> *An invitation to ride*
> *10 Hawking Road*
> *Midnight to Dawn*

"I don't get it." I looked at the bear as if it could give me an explanation, but all it gave me was a beady, red-eyed stare.

"Hey, Cassandra—" I turned to ask her what it was all about, but she was gone. Instead, the booth was now manned by some bearded, bald guy who looked like he'd rather be on a Harley than behind a counter.

"Three balls for a buck," he said. "Wanna play?"

"Wait a second. Where's Cassandra?"

"Cassandra who?"

I scanned the crowd around us, but there was no sign of her. Somewhere up above, the roller coaster plunged and the ground shook like an aftershock.

3
Ten and Two

Last month, on my sixteenth birthday, I bought a car with the money I had made working summer jobs for four years. Mom couldn't contribute, but that was okay, I never expected her to.

It's a Volvo. Beat up, rusty, and barely breathing, but a Volvo, nonetheless. Still the safest car on the road. Air bags, head-restraint system, front- and rear-end crumple zones, and a crush-resistant passenger compartment. No crash-test dummies lost their lives testing this one.

With my license only one month old, I drove us home from the amusement park with both hands on the wheel, positioned at ten and two, like we learned in driver's ed.

"What a rip!" Quinn complained. "What theme park closes at ten at night?" He fiddled with his nose ring, pulling loose a booger that had rotated out on the shiny silver ring like an asteroid. He wiped it on the dashboard, and I smacked him.

In the back Russ and Maggie examined the strange invitation to the phantom amusement park. "I think I've heard of this place," Maggie said. "If I'm right, it's supposed to be pretty good."

"I've heard of it too," Russ said.

I thought of the way Cassandra just disappeared. It was pretty creepy. "There's nothing down Hawking Road," I informed them. "Just the old quarry."

"Dude, it's a theme park rave. Never in the same place twice. Attendance by invitation only."

"And we've got an invitation," said Quinn.

"Correction: *I've* got an invitation."

Quinn made a face. "What good is it to you? You'll never go!"

"Maybe I will and maybe I won't." But we all knew I wouldn't. I turned a corner, arm over arm, then returned my hands to ten and two.

"You know what your problem is—" said Russ, but Maggie didn't let him finish the thought. She grabbed the invitation from him.

"If Blake doesn't want to go, then he doesn't have to go." She slipped the card back into the inbred bear's pocket. "It's probably overrated, anyway."

I held back a smile. Whenever I was at the short end of a disagreement, Maggie always shifted the balance to my side.

I dropped off Russ, then Maggie. As I worked my way through the neighborhood toward our house, Quinn set his mouth on cruise control, constantly complaining about how I came to a complete three-second stop at every stop sign.

"C'mon! At this time of night, stop signs are optional."

"Is there any rule that's not optional for you?"

Then, as I braked for the next stop sign, a little green car barreled across the intersection, completely ignoring the four-way stop.

"See? If I didn't stop, we would have smashed into that Pinto. Do you know what happens when you hit a Pinto?"

"What?"

"They blow up!"

"Cool!" said Quinn.

As it turned out, explosive Pintos were the least of our problems. I could tell what type of evening it was going to be when we drove up to our house and saw Mom out front with Carl, boyfriend of the month.

So you get the complete picture, I ought to explain about my mother and her boyfriends. You see, Mom is sort of like a blue whale. I don't mean she's big—she's actually on the small side. What I mean is that Mom filters losers through her baleen as if they were krill. I don't know why; she's a good person with a big heart—enough of a heart to raise Quinn and me alone on what little she makes. But when it comes to herself, I don't know, it's like she never aims as high as she deserves. She could have graduated college, but she dropped out because Dad wanted her to. Then when Dad left, she never went back, because she had to support us.

Most of the guys she's dated were like Dad. They drank too much, demanded too much, and when it came time to give something back, they bailed. But her latest boyfriend seemed to be an exception to the rule. Aside from a bad hair transplant that looked like rows of wheat and a wardrobe that was just a bit too young for him, Carl seemed to be an okay guy. But I reserve judgment on anyone Mom filters through her baleen.

Now, as I drove up, Carl had a new mark against him, because he was making out with Mom on the porch—and I mean *really* making out, the way I should have been doing at around this time in my life. I was thankful we'd dropped Maggie and Russ off already so they didn't have to witness the scene.

"Now, *that's* what I call a vomit ride," I told Quinn as we pulled up the driveway. He snickered. No matter what disagreements we had, we were of one mind when it came to Mom and her boyfriends.

As soon as we got out of the car, they stopped sucking face. Mom looked embarrassed at having been caught.

"Hi, guys," Carl said. He noticed the bear I held. "Looks like you came up a winner."

"Carl was just saying good-bye," Mom said.

"Really," I said. "He must speak in tongues."

That got me a high five from Quinn. When we were done laughing, Mom raised her eyebrows and said, "Are you done having your joke at our expense?"

Oh, please don't try to sound parental now. "Yeah. Sorry."

"Good, because Carl and I have an announcement to make." She took his hand, and I felt my gut beginning to collapse into a knot, because I knew what she was going to say. I knew because of the ring I saw on her hand. It was a diamond; and I had a feeling it was no cheap zircon, either, but the real thing. I clenched the arm of the misshapen bear tighter.

"We're engaged," she said, and bounced up and down like a cheerleader. Her enthusiasm was met by our silence. "Well, aren't you going to congratulate us?"

Frankly I didn't know what I felt: good, bad, or indifferent. The news hadn't completely sunk in yet. But Quinn took it all in at once. First his ears went red, and the redness spread like a rash across his pinched face.

"Well?" Mom prompted.

"The last guy's ring was bigger," Quinn said, and tried to storm off into the house. Carl grabbed Quinn by the arm, and Quinn braced himself to be hit. It was a natural reflex after years of Mom's boyfriends, who spoke in fists rather than in tongues. But Carl, to his credit, wasn't like that. He only grabbed Quinn to get his attention, and he let go as soon as he had.

"Hey," he said, "I've got something for you, Quinn." He held out a small jewelry box, flipping it open to reveal a tiny diamond ear stud. It was just like the one Carl himself wore.

"I don't want it."

"Take it, Quinn," Mom said. It was an order.

Carl cautiously took a step closer to Quinn. "Here, let me." He removed the sputnik dangling from Quinn's ear, replacing it with the diamond stud. "Sometimes one is enough, when it's the right one."

Quinn grimaced like he was having a root canal.

Finally Carl stepped back. The new stud was still one among three earrings in his ear, but it was definitely less in-your-face than the sputnik.

"Can I go now?" Quinn didn't wait for an answer. He bolted into the house, slamming the screen door behind him.

Carl sighed. "Well, that could have been worse." Then he looked at me. I was still feeling numb about the whole thing, but I knew what I had to say to get me out of this awkward situation.

"I'm very happy for you both." I turned to go in.

"Carl has something for you, too," Mom said.

"It's okay," I told them. "I'm not Quinn. I don't need a bribe." The words slipped out before I could hold them back.

"It's not like that, Blake," Carl said. "I know we're going to be family. . . . But I want to be friends, too."

I cringed at the word *family*. For years our little family had been about as misshapen as the bear I was holding. It didn't need more stuffing, it needed a complete makeover. The guys Mom dragged into the task never made it through the preliminaries. Was Carl so different? Did I want him to be?

Carl reached into his sports jacket and produced an overstuffed envelope. He held it out to me, a gesture of friendship. "Just some things you might need at college," he said, "and some phone numbers of friends I have in the city. New York can be rough without someone to help you out."

I took it, thanked him, and went inside, riding a wave

of sudden nausea—a sort of seasickness from the many unexpected lurches of the evening. They say it's not the sideways motion of a ship that makes you sick, but the pitch and yaw: the constant rising and falling of the bow, both predictable and yet different with every wave. On days like this, it felt like I'd never get used to it.

Once in the house, I spared one more look at the ungainly little bear and his unpleasant yellow shirt. It was my trophy for a twisted evening that wasn't getting any better. The corner of the invitation stuck out of the bear's pocket, but I didn't care about that anymore. I wasn't going. Cassandra would probably be there, but who was I kidding? She was out of my league.

On the way to my room I passed Quinn's closed door. Angry music blared on the other side. I just didn't feel like dealing with him, or his room. I mean, imagine the debris field of a tornado, and you'll begin to understand what it looked like. There were dust bunnies that lurked in corners, evolving into higher forms of life. Half-eaten sandwiches growing thick green fur filled the bookshelves.

No surprise that my room looked nothing like my brother's. I opened my door to a clean floor, a neat desk, and a host of evenly spaced travel posters lining the walls. Russia, England, and Greece hung over my desk. Above my headboard was Italy, with the Leaning Tower of Pisa, and on my closet door was France, with the Eiffel Tower and the Arc De Triomphe looking like a hundred-foot keyhole into all the places I'd never been. An oversized poster of Hawaii was strategically placed as a backdrop for some World War II model planes I'd hung from the ceiling in a mock dogfight.

The posters had been free because they knew me at the travel agency down at the mall. When I was younger, I hung out there, and they would pretend to book me on trips to faraway places. Then they'd give me the posters, along with whatever other promotional stuff was lying around in their office. That was how I got the two carved heads from Easter Island that now served as bookends and an authentic imitation totem pole from Alaska that stood in the corner.

My desk was empty except for a desk organizer holding paper clips, pens, and sharpened pencils. Quinn called it "anal" the way I kept everything, as if being neat were some weird complex. As if there were something wrong with having all my pencils sharpened and my books in alphabetical order and my clothes hung up by color. So what? I used to do that with my crayons, too.

I sat at my desk and opened the envelope Carl had given me. Like he said, it contained a list of names and phone numbers of people I didn't know in New York, but there were other things in it as well. Like a subway map I couldn't figure out no matter which way I held it. Like a brochure from Columbia University's sports department that featured the school mascot, a menacing blue lion, stalking forward as if trying to intimidate me out of trying out for their swim team.

And then there were the airplane tickets.

American Airlines. 6:45 A.M. departure. September 4. One was round-trip, for my mom. She got to stay for two days. The other ticket was mine and was one-way. The flight landed at an airport called LaGuardia. I'd never flown—never had the need to—but now here was a ticket, with a date only one month away.

Ever have the real world hit you like a steel pole to the head? Until now all I had from the university was an acceptance letter and a dozen forms to fill out. But here, spread out before me, was solid reality on a collision course with me. *Wham!* Sixteen years old and living at a college in New York City? What was I, crazy? Was I totally out of my mind? My head was spinning, and whenever that happened, it always called back that memory of my first ride.

Screaming. Spinning out of control. Gripping tightly on to the seat. So dizzy . . .

Too tired to resist, I let the memory come. I was seven. There are so many details I still remember, like the smell of cherry-flavored bubble gum in the air and the cold feel of the seat and the screams of my friends, each voice a different pitch, like a terrified choir, all out of tune. And yet so much is also gone. Not so much forgotten as exiled from my brain. Maybe that's because the ride didn't take place at a carnival or an amusement park. It took place on an icy December morning. On a school bus.

Mom never talked about it, and so neither did I. I always figured the memory of that ride was best left buried. Problem is, rides like that have a way of coming back, and then you're stuck riding them again. And again. And again.

I brought my hands to my temples, pressing until the spinning feeling went away. Then I took the subway map, the list of names, and the brochure, and dropped them in the trash. I made sure the brochure was face-down, so I wouldn't have to see the eyes of that blue lion. As for the plane tickets, I shoved them as far and as deep in my desk as I could, knowing I really couldn't throw them away but wishing that I could at least make them disappear.

I went to the kitchen as Mom came inside.

"Did you look in the packet Carl gave you?"

"I'm tired, Mom. Can we talk about it in the morning?"

I scavenged through the fridge, finding doggie bags left over from her and Carl's big engagement date. Wan Fu's Szechuan Emporium: the most expensive Chinese restaurant in town. At least the guy had good taste in food.

Mom leaned against the wall. "Why does Quinn have to be like this? It's like I'm not allowed to have any happiness around here."

I didn't feel like getting into it. "Not everything's about you, Mom."

"Yeah, well, not everything's about him, either."

I snatched up the doggie bags, and instead of escaping to my clean room, I went in Quinn's pigsty. At least there, the chaos was all out in the open, instead of hiding in unseen places.

I pushed open his door. A dart zipped through the air headed straight for my face. I deflected it with the doggie bags, and it punctured the flaming *Hindenburg* on Quinn's classic Led Zeppelin poster instead, which had once been Mom's until retro became cool and Quinn nabbed it.

"That would have been a bull's-eye," Quinn complained. I looked at the dartboard on the back of the door.

"Fat chance. It wouldn't even have hit the target."

Quinn shrugged and turned his attention to a flight simulation game on his computer. It was typical Quinn: playing darts while playing computer games while blasting music loud enough to shake the house from its foundation. I turned down the music a few hundred decibels so I could hear myself think, as Quinn ditched his plane in a cornfield.

"Isn't the object to actually *land* the plane?"

"Where's the fun in that?" Quinn quit the game and flopped bonelessly onto his bed. I sat on his desk chair, handing him one of the bags of food. "Here, stuff your face. Mom and Carl had Chinese."

"Great! They're engaged five minutes, and we're already eating his table scraps." He riffled around his desk until he found a fork with dried ketchup on it and started eating.

I studied the diamond stud in Quinn's earlobe. "I like it better than sputnik," I told him.

Quinn looked at me as if I'd insulted him. "*You* gave me sputnik."

"Yeah, but when I gave it to you, it was a key chain."

He returned to his food. Lo mein noodles dangled from his chin like worms as he sucked them in. "You watch," Quinn said. "This guy's going to bail, and we'll never hear from him again. Just like the other ones . . ."

I looked away. He didn't have to say it—I knew what he was thinking: *Just like Dad.*

I wanted to reach out to Quinn somehow, but I couldn't. It made me think of this thing I once read. Scientists now think there are actually nine dimensions instead of three, but the other ones are so folded in upon themselves, we can't experience them. Maybe that explains why I could never reach out to Quinn, because although he was only a few feet away, he somehow felt much farther than the space between us. When Dad left us all those years ago, it tore open a wound that led to a whole lot of unexpected dimensions.

"Hey, maybe this guy'll hang around," I said. "And maybe it won't be so bad."

"Easy for you to say. You'll be off at Columbia."

I felt the skin on the back of my neck tighten. "I never said I was going."

Quinn laughed, his mouth full of noodles. "Yeah, right. You're gonna turn down an Ivy League scholarship."

When I didn't answer him, his expression changed.

"Wait a second. You're not kidding!"

I began to pace, kicking the debris on the floor out of the way. "That scholarship doesn't cover everything. And do you know how expensive New York is?"

"One month to go, and you're gonna talk yourself out of it?"

"I'm being practical. I know *that* particular word never made it into your vocabulary."

Quinn put down his fork. "You're chicken, aren't you?"

"It's better for everyone if I get a part-time job and take some classes at a junior college."

But Quinn wasn't buying it. "You're scared! I can't believe you. I mean, you paste your room full of places you'll never go, and when you actually get the chance to have a life, you're too scared to take it!"

He had a point. But so did I. "If I go to junior college, I can live at home," I reminded him, "and maybe keep some balance around here. Besides, you never know when someone might need their ass saved from a roller coaster again."

"Oh, right. So it's my fault?"

"Do you really want to face life with the newlyweds alone? What if they do crash and burn?"

"You mean like you're doing now?" Quinn crushed a fortune cookie in his fist and let the flakes fall away. "Fine! See if I care. Go turn your life into a car accident. Or should I say a *bus* accident?"

I spun to face him, feeling his words like a slap. So he did know! But to use his knowledge against me like that—it was unforgivable.

"Accident?" I said. "No, Quinn. *You're* the only 'accident' in this family!"

I regretted it the moment I said it, but it was too late. I couldn't take it back. Quinn's expression hardened into hate, and I braced myself for a serious verbal beating. But instead, he broke eye contact, looking down at the mess on the ground. He brushed the cookie flakes from his hand, pulling out the fortune.

"Hey, don't worry about me, bro," he said, waving his fortune. "It says here YOU ARE EMPEROR OF ALL YOU SURVEY." He crumpled the paper into a ball and flicked it away.

I wanted to say something to him. An apology, maybe, but it was like I'd just thrown a stone at a glass house and the shards were still falling all around me. I just had to get out, so I went to my room and lay down on the taut blanket of my perfectly made bed, looking up at the Parthenon and the Eiffel Tower and the Kremlin and the Great Wall of China—things that existed somewhere out there in one of the many dimensions I knew I'd never have access to. Things that were all so frighteningly far away.

Screaming. Spinning out of control. Gripping tightly on to the seat. So dizzy . . .

I am there again. I am seven, on a school bus, spinning. Crashing through the guardrail, caught on the edge of the canyon now, balanced like a teeter-totter, tilting, tilting. Me, crawling down the aisle, toward the emergency exit at the back. The floor rising like a black wave before me as the front end of the bus tilts forward, and I'm climbing the rising floor toward the back of the bus. Pounding, pounding, pounding the emergency exit door. A teacher screaming, "Open it, Blake." What's her name? I can't remember. I'm hitting the door, banging, kicking. I'm not strong enough to open it. I'm not strong enough to open the emergency exit door.

The floor of the bus is a rising wave. The wave hits. It swallows me.

★ ★ ★

My eyes shot open, and I shivered uncontrollably until the warmth of my room brought my mind and body back from the nightmare. It was two o'clock in the morning—definitely not my favorite time to be awake. The dream was fading, but something wasn't right. Strange light flashed through the blinds, casting shifting slits of light on my travel posters. I sat up and looked out of the window.

An ambulance was parked on our driveway.

"He was just lying there on the living room floor," Mom was telling the paramedics as I came out of my room. "I couldn't wake him up."

It was Quinn.

They had him on the couch now, but he wasn't moving. One of the two guys shone a light into Quinn's eyes and checked his pulse.

"Accelerated pulse. Eyes fixed and dilated," he said. "Do you know what he was on?"

What he was "on"? The question infuriated me. "He wasn't 'on' anything," I said. They turned to see me there for the first time. "Quinn doesn't do drugs."

But he does other things, I thought. *Things that can get into his bloodstream as quickly as drugs. Things that are just as addictive. He does acceleration instead of speed.*

But I didn't tell them that, and they just looked at me, not believing me. Not even Mom. She ran off to check his drawers for whatever stash he might have.

The paramedics lifted Quinn onto a gurney, and as

they did, something fell off the couch: a stuffed bear with a lopsided head wearing a yellow shirt with a pocket. I picked up the bear. The pocket was empty. The invitation was gone.

There was a logical, sensible explanation for that—there had to be—but I wasn't feeling sensible at that moment. I hurried over to Quinn. His eyes were half open as if he were dead, but he was still breathing. It was as if Quinn weren't really there. His body was, but Quinn himself was gone.

I go places sometimes.

"Where did you go, Quinn?" I said aloud. "Where did you go?" And as I peered into his eyes I got something of an answer.

Because reflected from the shine of his wide pupils I could see lights—spinning carnival lights, and I could swear I heard the faint echoes of calliope music and screams.

The paramedics shouldered me out of the way and rolled Quinn out the door.

4

True Void

I'm not the kind of guy to make huge leaps into the impossible. I don't believe in aliens, I have no faith in psychics, and tales of the Loch Ness monster leave me cold. So I can't begin to explain what made me believe that Quinn had stolen my invitation and taken some sort of spiritual road trip to God-knows-where. Call it unwanted intuition, but whatever it was, I simply knew.

"It's not that we don't believe you, Blake," Maggie said. "It's just that you need to see this from our side."

By twenty past two I was in the Volvo with Russ and Maggie, because I knew I couldn't face this trip alone. I had driven to their houses and woken them up with long blasts of my horn—woken up half the neighborhood, I imagine—and practically dragged them out of bed.

"You wanted to go," I'd told them. "Now you've got your chance."

I slammed my brakes at a stop sign. Russ and Maggie jolted forward from the backseat, their seat belts digging into their shoulders.

"Thanks. That woke me up," said Russ.

"This is crazy," Maggie said. "I mean, you've put two and two together and come up with pi."

I floored the accelerator and pulled through the intersection. "You didn't see Quinn's eyes. I'm telling you, he wasn't *there*. Maybe his body was, but *he* wasn't. Don't ask me how to explain it, but somehow he's at that freaking amusement park."

"You mean like an out-of-body experience?" Maggie asked.

"I don't know! I just know he's there." I screeched to a halt at the next stop sign, then hurled forward again.

"I think *I* just had an out-of-body experience," Russ said.

"But . . . if he went there in his *head*," Maggie asked, "how are we supposed to get there in a *Volvo*?"

"All I know is that we had an invitation to an address on Hawking Road. It's the only clue we have, so I'm following it."

I turned onto the deserted stretch of Hawking Road. It wound through a forest, leading nowhere anyone would ever want to go.

Maggie put her hand on my shoulder. Russ was too tired to even notice. "Listen," she said, "we'll get there, and you'll see it's just a carnival. Then we can all drive to the hospital and wait to find out what's up with Quinn." She spoke to me like someone talking to a leaper on a ledge. Well, maybe she was right. The best thing that could happen to me was to prove that I was a deranged idiot. It was better than the alternative.

We passed a sign that said SPEED LIMIT 45. From

habit, I looked down at the speedometer. The pin wavered at 45. That wouldn't do. I extended my foot and watched as our speed passed 50.

"Blake," said Russ. "You're speeding."

"I know."

"All right. *Now* I'm scared."

Up ahead a wooden sign nailed to a tree bore a red symbol—a wave intersecting a spiral—just like the one on the invitation. An arrow pointed to the left, down a dirt road, and I took a sharp turn, feeling the car almost lose its grip on the asphalt. The smoothness of the paved road gave way to bone-jarring, uneven bumps. Deep down, I knew this place we were headed wasn't really an amusement park.

Am I nuts? Am I nuts to think what I'm thinking?

"Watch out!" screamed Maggie.

Suddenly the road took a sharp turn, and a huge oak tree loomed in my headlights. I spun the wheel and stomped on the brake. The wheels lost traction, and the car narrowly missed the tree. We careened through the underbrush until finally the car skidded to a halt.

I shut my eyes for a moment and took a deep breath, trying to pull myself together. Somehow everything around me felt different in some fundamental way that's still hard to describe. You know how when there's a noise that's so constant, you forget there's any noise at all? Like the hum of an air conditioner? You don't notice the sound until it's gone, and then, for a moment, the *deeper* silence is so eerily empty, your brain kind of gets thrown off balance. That's the best way I can describe what I felt as I sat there behind the wheel—only it wasn't just sound, it was every other sense as well. It was like ripping through the normal fabric of life's noise into a true void.

I stepped out of the car. We'd come to a stop just short of a canyon rim. There before us was the old quarry, which had been shut down for years. Only now it didn't look much like a quarry. The crevasse below was a fog-filled rift, glowing with colored lights. I could smell cotton candy and popcorn. I could hear the sound of grinding gears, punctuated by the ghostly echoes of screaming riders. In the center of the breach I could see the very top of a Ferris wheel rising above the fog, churning the moonlit mist like a riverboat paddle.

"I think we've all gone schizo," Russ said, holding Maggie tightly, as if she were the one who was unnerved.

I turned at the sound of nearby laughter. Other kids. Where had they come from? They sifted through the woods, invitations in hand, descending a path down into the canyon. *Was this how Quinn came here?* I wondered. *Was this ridge some interface between mind and matter, and were all these kids actually lying unconscious somewhere?* I hadn't seen any other cars, and this place was too far out of the way to walk. But that would mean . . . No. I didn't want to think about it.

With my friends close behind, I joined the other kids in the procession toward the park.

Russ looked at the narrow, winding path down into the crevasse. "How do you suppose they got all those rides down there? You think there's a back road?"

Neither Maggie nor I answered him.

"I mean, it was a quarry, right? There has to be a road. . . ."

We came through the layer of fog. There before us was the entrance to the park. Ticket booths and turnstiles. Pretty ordinary, except for the fact that every theme park I've ever been to has its name written on all available surfaces, from benches to soda cups, just in case you might forget where you are. This park didn't seem to have a name.

"I'll need to see your invitations," a cashier demanded as we came to his booth. He had a little computer console but no cash register. The guy didn't look too healthy. He was kind of malnourished and crater-eyed. His skin was so pale, it looked like he hadn't seen the sun in a long time.

I pretended to check my pockets. "Wouldn't you know it. It's in my other pants."

"Sorry," the cashier said. "No one gets in without an invitation."

I leaned in close to him. "Listen, my kid brother stole it, and I have to get in there and kick his butt."

Suddenly he stiffened, putting a hand to his ear. That's when I noticed he was wearing one of those earpieces. You know, the kind that the secret service wear. He listened to something in his earphone. "Yes," he said. "All right."

Russ tapped me on the shoulder and whispered uneasily, "Look at that earpiece."

Only then did I notice that the wire from the earphone

didn't wrap around his ear. It went directly into his head. I suppressed a shiver.

The cashier turned to us. "You have permission to enter."

"Permission from whom?"

"If you have to ask, then you haven't met her."

"Maybe I have."

He punched some keys on the computer. "It looks like your brother's been inside for an hour."

So there it was. Confirmation. I looked to Maggie and Russ. There was surprise in their faces but not all that much. Deep down, they had known, just as I had.

"So will you be riding with us today or not?" the cashier asked impatiently.

I nodded. "I'll ride."

"We all will," Maggie said. She pulled Russ forward, who, big talker that he was, suddenly had cold feet for this amusement park.

"Alrighty, then," said the cashier. "Take a look at your right hand."

I looked down. The wave-and-spiral symbol was branded in red across the back of my hand. Maggie and Russ had the symbol too.

"Where'd that come from?" Maggie asked.

"Trick of the trade," the cashier answered.

"Yeah, but can he pull a coin out of an ear?" Russ said nervously.

At the suggestion the cashier glanced at Russ thoughtfully, as if he might actually shove a hand through his ear and pull a coin out of Russ's brain.

"Run your hand across the scanners in the park to activate a turnstile," the cashier said. "The mark is good for seven rides. No more, no less. You can't leave the park until you ride all seven, and you've got to do it by dawn. Did you get that? Is there any part of that you don't understand? Do I need to repeat it?"

"Our hands activate the turnstiles, and we have to ride seven rides by dawn. Got it."

"Dawn today is at 6 A.M. That gives you more than three hours. Enjoy yourselves."

"What happens if we're not done by dawn?" Russ asked, but the cashier had already shifted his attention to the next people in line.

Before us stood the arched entrance, painted with the bright trappings of amusement. Happy faces and balloons. The promise of thrills. The iron gate was open wide, and a force pulled us toward the arch, as if the ground were at an awkward tilt. Other excited guests pushed in front of us to get through. I thought about Quinn. Somewhere in the outside world Quinn's body was being shuttled through an emergency room, pored over by doctors, but nothing they could do would help him, because he wasn't there. His mind and his spirit were here, and I had to go in, body and soul, to bring him back.

I turned to my friends. "You don't have to come," I told them. "He's *my* brother."

Maggie looked at the entry gate. I could see she was afraid, but she pushed the fear back. If we stepped through the gate, I knew the last threads of sanity that bound together the world we knew, the real world, would pull part. I could almost feel my fingers holding tightly on to those threads, ready to pull on them and make them all unravel.

"Are you kidding?" Maggie said. "Let you ride all alone?"

"Yeah," said Russ, glancing around anxiously, as if already looking for a way out. "We're here for you, pal."

I turned toward the flashing lights and led us under the arch, crossing the threshold into the park with no name.

5

Carousel

"So what's the big deal?"

Russ was unimpressed by the place, and kind of relieved. I can't say that I blamed him. There was one main path winding through the park with rides on either side. To our right was a mural of a tall ship lurching on a wild sea, its sails shredded by a storm. The once-bright colors had faded, and the peeling paint revealed warping plywood beneath. Beyond the mural was the swinging boat ride it advertised: a miniature ship, swinging back and forth on a single axle—a typical carnival ride. In fact, everything seemed typical. There was a pint-size bumper car arena, a carousel piping out calliope music, and any number of spinning rides. Each one was the kind of attraction that could easily be taken down and reassembled in a day.

Russ picked at the peeling paint of the ocean mural. "This is nothing but a kiddie park."

I began to doubt the intuition that led me here. Maybe my mind had connected the dots and found an unlikely pattern, the way people once looked at the stars and found the figures of gods in the constellations. Maybe the lights spinning in Quinn's eyes had just been a reflection of the ambulance lights. Maybe this place was exactly what it claimed to be and the cashier mentioning my brother was just making it up. I found myself wanting to believe that more and more.

To our right a black-and-white eggbeater ride picked up speed. It was a Tilt-A-Whirl with eight spinning arms. At the end of each arm a pair of pods revolved around each other, and in each of the pods disoriented riders screamed with the thrill of the speed.

Maggie was the first to notice something strange. "Look at them," she said. "What's wrong with them?"

I caught glimpses of the kids on the ride as they swooped past. Their faces were blurry, and the color of their clothes bled off into the air around them, until the ride spun so fast that I couldn't see them anymore. No ride I'd ever seen could move that fast! Then all at once the lights on the ride went out. The hydraulic pistons that held the revolving cars in the air began to hiss, bringing the pods back down to the ground. When the ride beat itself to a halt, the pods were empty. The riders were gone. Lap bars popped up with a clang; the lights of the ride flickered back on. A new crew of excited riders hurried to take their seats.

"Maybe we'll pass on the particle accelerator," Russ said, backing away. If we had any doubts as to the nature of this place, they were gone now. We were all believers—although I wasn't quite sure what we were being asked to believe.

Maggie gripped Russ's arm. I could see her nails practically digging into his skin, but she was looking at me.

"Don't get on it, Blake," she said.

"I don't intend to." I looked at the new riders taking their seats, pulling down the lap bars, waiting for the ride to start. I wondered if they saw what had happened to the riders before them. Were they so blinded by their own excitement that they couldn't see? Or didn't they care?

"What do you suppose happened to them?" Maggie asked. "Where do you suppose they went?"

"I think it's best if we don't suppose anything."

I turned away from the ride as it started up again. *I'm here for a reason,* I told myself. *My stinking lousy brother is here.* If I remembered that, then maybe I'd keep from losing my mind.

We walked into a crowd of kids. I'm pretty tall and could see over almost everyone. Far up ahead I spotted a kid wearing a black hat, walking away from me. Earrings dangled from his left ear. Was it Quinn? I was too far away to tell. I bolted forward, but once I'd fought my way through the crowd, the kid with the hat was nowhere to be seen. Had he dissolved into the park too, or did he just get lost in the mob? There was no telling. For an instant I felt the earth shifting beneath me, tilting to the left and to the right. It was only me. My equilibrium had been thrown off by the crowds, the lights, and the sound of gears grinding louder than the music that echoed around me. I turned to look for Russ and Maggie, but I instead caught sight of a girl with copper hair, watching me from a distance.

Cassandra.

She wasn't flirting. She just seemed to be observing. Studying me. Although she stood in the midst of the moving masses, their footsteps avoided her, as if she were in a protective bubble. As if space itself were warped around her. She was more than just an agent of this place, passing out invitations. Even from this distance, I could feel a sense of . . . of *propriety* about her. *This place is hers,* I realized. I don't know how I knew that, but I did.

She held my gaze for an instant, then turned, sauntering through the parting crowd toward the carousel, as if daring me to follow.

I took the dare.

"Blake. Don't!"

I felt Maggie's hand on my shoulder, but I pulled away, making my way as fast as I could to the carousel. I hit the turnstile. It snagged me painfully at the waist, not giving way. I pushed at it again until I realized why it held me back. I looked at my hand. The red symbol was glowing white-hot; I could feel its heat on my skin. I ran my hand across the scanner, and the glow faded to a smoldering crimson. The turnstile let me through. Ahead of me the carousel had already begun to move.

"Cassandra!"

I jumped on the ride, grabbing a pole as the carousel animals slowly began to rise and fall. She was standing on the far side of the platform, still scrutinizing me. I caught a glimpse of her smile and then lost sight of her among the riders and the herd of brightly painted animals. And what strange animals they were. The carousel had every nature of beast painted in loud, unexpected colors. There was a purple and yellow wolverine baring its teeth and a green and yellow ram, its wooden head down and ready to charge. I saw what looked like an anteater, blue and gold, looking absurd as it rose and fell with the rhythm of the ride. And yet, as strange as these animals appeared, they were also somehow familiar.

At the core of the ride was an array of mirrors. I felt if I could focus on any one of those mirrors long enough, I'd see Cassandra staring out at me. The carousel picked up speed, and when I came around near the turnstile again, Russ and Maggie leaped on.

"Let's just grab Blake and get off," Russ told Maggie.

But I wasn't looking at Russ. I was looking at the purple and gray tiger behind him, at how its wooden eyes appeared to track his movements. The creature right in front of me was a menacing lion painted bright blue. Was it my imagination, or was its snarling mouth an inch wider than it had been a moment ago? The ride picked up more speed. The tempo of the carnival music accelerated, rising to the highest octaves. I could feel centrifugal force pushing me outward and—what was that I saw? Were the legs of these painted animals actually beginning to move?

All at once the wooden floorboards began to buckle and give, revealing a rocky terrain rushing beneath us.

"Grab on to something!" I shouted. "It's coming apart!" As the floorboards fell away I leaped onto the animal closest to me, the blue lion. Maggie took the green and yellow ram, and Russ found himself an oversized gray and blue peacock. I gripped the pole, but the pole disappeared between my fingers. The last of the floorboards disintegrated. My blue lion opened his mouth, releasing a thunderous roar that resonated up my legs and into my chest. And finally I realized where I'd seen all these creatures before.

They were all college mascots.

Now the last thread that held the world together unraveled, and I plunged through its shredded fragments into a wholly different place. The ride had come undone—it had *unfolded*—into an endless rocky plain beneath a red sky and an eclipsed sun. I was riding through this unearthly landscape, clinging to the mane of a blue lion, surrounded by hundreds of other beasts. Some creatures had riders. Others didn't. But every single one of them was a mascot. I knew them from sports and from TV, but mostly I knew them from the endless applications I had filled out to dozens of universities far from home.

It was all I could do to stay on the lion, for although it now moved with the agility of flesh, to the touch it was still like slippery, painted wood. All of these animals were a strange melding of wood, paint, and flesh.

Who made this place?

Beside me I passed an unfortunate boy desperately trying to get some speed out of the banana slug he rode. From behind him, what could only be described as a Fighting Irishman grabbed him by the scruff of his collar.

"Outta me way," the Irishman said, and hurled the kid off his slug so far out of sight that I had no idea where he landed.

It's only a ride, I told myself. *It's only a ride.*

I caught up to Maggie on her ram. She was experienced on horseback and had taken to the shape and rhythm of her new mount. The look on her face wasn't fear; it was something slowly creeping toward ecstasy.

"This is wild!" she said as I passed her.

My lion leaped over a rock, and I rose off his back, coming down on his haunches, practically at the tail. I had to throw all my weight forward to keep from falling off.

"You'll never make it if you ride like that."

It was Cassandra. She rode a huge beast the color of blood that matched pace with my lion. It was a razorback, but it was more dinosaur than hog. Cassandra wasn't dressed in the clothes she'd worn before but was in some exotic safari outfit. And as I looked at myself I saw that I was wearing the same thing. In fact, everyone was. It was as if costumes were part of the deal here.

"None of this is real!" I shouted to her. "It can't be! I'm getting off!"

"Bad idea."

As I looked ahead of me I saw what she meant. There was a kid on an orange longhorn bull who was having as much trouble as I was. I heard him scream as he slipped off the bull, but his screams were silenced under the trampling feet of the stampede.

"You could call this the weed-out course," Cassandra said with a dry smile.

"Okay," I said, hugging the neck of my lion. "Okay. I get the idea. You can stop the ride now."

She laughed at me. "The ride doesn't stop. Find your way to another ride. That's the only way to get off."

Another ride? That implied surviving this one. Had Quinn been through this? He would have loved it! He would have *died* loving it!

"Where's my brother?"

Instead of answering, Cassandra tugged on the ears of her razorback. It turned its head, opened its massive jaw, and dug its tusks into my lion, shredding its neck.

"*Bad* piggy," Cassandra said, but it was clear this was exactly what she had intended to do. Maggie came up behind me. Her ram reared and threw her to the ground. My lion roared in pain, wood splintering in all directions. It collapsed, and I tumbled off just as the huge razorback chomped down on my lion, lifted it up, and swallowed it whole.

"Survival of the fittest," Cassandra said with a wink. "Looks like your lion didn't make the grade." Then she rode off, leaving me and Maggie standing in the middle of the stampede.

"We're toast," Maggie said.

By now I'd seen more than one kid trampled into dust. *What happens if you die here?* I wondered. *Is it just the end of the ride, or something worse?*

"Come on!" I grabbed Maggie's hand and wove us through the stampede. Somehow we managed to sidestep every animal. I turned away from the kid being swallowed by a crimson alligator and another who got speared by a maroon and gold Trojan warrior. We fought our way past a host of horrors until we came out into tall grass. I was exhausted, but I felt I could run forever to get away from this place.

"Wait! What about Russ?" Maggie said. We'd completely forgotten about him.

I turned back, fearing the worst. But he, too, had broken away from the stampede—only he hadn't left his mount. He still rode the back of that gargantuan peacock, which now ran AWOL through the grass.

"Help!" Russ yelled. "Get me off this thing!" As big as he was, he was at the mercy of the ridiculous bird.

Maggie and I ran toward him, just as his bird reached the edge of a gully and lost its balance. It tumbled, disappearing down the ravine along with Russ. By the time we got to him, Russ was already picking himself up out of the dust. He was fine, but the peacock wasn't.

"I broke my bird." It lay in splinters around him. The bird's wooden head and neck were still intact, pecking at Russ's ankles. He kicked it away in disgust.

Now that the ride was over, my legs gave out, and I had to sit down on a boulder. I looked at my hands, my feet, the ground around me. I looked at the boulders and at the bright red sky. Nothing I had experienced before stepping on that carousel had prepared me for this. I knew it couldn't be happening, and yet it seemed so real—*more* than real. There was a heightened sense of reality to everything around us, as if this place truly *was* made up of whole new dimensions beyond the three that filled up the rest of our lives. My senses were so unaccustomed to it, I didn't know whether to feel wonder or terror.

Maggie came up beside me. "You okay?"

"Why are you asking *him*?" said Russ. "What about *me*? I'm a wreck! I want to go home! I didn't sign up for some weird, communal acid trip."

But Russ was wrong to call it that. This was the exact opposite of some drugged-out experience. We still had our senses. Our minds were sharp and clear. It was the rest of the world that had gone crazy.

"The rules have changed," I told them. "We've got to accept it and learn to deal with things the way they are now."

I stood up, feeling my strength return and feeling my senses adapting to the dimensions of this new reality. "It's kind of like learning to swim. The first time you were in water, it must have felt like this."

"So we've got to learn to swim through this place?"

"Either we make all the right moves, or we drown."

Russ shook his head quickly, nervously. "No. No. We've just got to stop this."

Maggie ignored him and turned to me. "Who was that girl on the killer pig? You talked to her like you knew her."

"You know her too. She ran the ball-toss booth. She was the one who gave us the invitation."

"Gave *you* the invitation," Russ said. "*I* wasn't invited. *I* should get to go home."

"You heard what that guy at the entrance said,"

Maggie reminded him. "We can't get out until we ride seven rides."

Russ started pacing in circles like a gorilla in a cage. "I don't get this ride, anyway. I mean, what's with these weird animals?"

"I don't think you're supposed to get it," I told him. "I think . . ." I hesitated. "I think it's for me. You're just along for the ride."

"What? How could they make an entire ride just for you?" Maggie asked.

"Not they—*her*. Cassandra." The more I thought about it, the more sure I was that she was at the bottom of it all. "It's like she gets inside your head somehow. She takes what she finds there and whips it up into this."

The thought stopped Russ in midpace. "Well, dude, maybe I don't want some witch-chick picking the corners of my brain."

I forced a smirk. "Why? Y'think she'll find something there besides toe-jam?"

"Hey, you've got rides you'd rather skip, and so do I." He looked up to the red sky as if some rescue might come by helicopter. "We'll find her, and we'll bargain our way out. That's what we'll do."

But I already knew what I had to do. "No. We go on to the next ride."

"You've picked a hell of a time to grow some guts," he said. "Do us all a favor and go back to being a coward."

I could have hit him for that. I could have hit him and hurt him; and although he was stronger than me back home, I knew things were different here. This *place* was different. Here, it seemed muscle wasn't made of flesh and blood; it was made of will and anger. And at that moment I had enough strength to hurl him into the eclipsed sun.

Maggie came between us like a referee. "You know," she said, "maybe I'm crazy, but I sort of liked the ride."

Russ just looked at her. "*Liked* it?"

"It's an amusement park, right? Maybe we should try to enjoy it."

Russ strode over to a slim boulder about as tall as he was. "Really? Why don't you ask *this* guy if he's enjoying it?"

"What do you mean?" Then, as I looked at the boulder, I understood. It wasn't exactly in the form of a person, but the boulder did seem to have sagging shoulders and smooth indentations that could have been eyes and a mouth, if the light hit it just right. In fact, all the boulders around gave us the uncanny impression of human figures hunched by the weight of the granite.

"Somehow," I told my friends, "I don't think any of this is for our amusement."

"All the more reason to cut a deal with the Queen of Mean and get out," Russ said.

"You do what you want, but I'm finding Quinn."

Russ threw up his hands. "What is it with you that you've got to save *his* butt before your own?"

"He's my brother."

Then Maggie looked at me. "I think it's more than that, isn't it?"

I hesitated for a moment. Was it more than that? The

thing is, I was the one who had pushed Quinn over the edge. I'd called him a human accident, knowing how much it would hurt him. If I hadn't said it, would he have come here? Maybe, maybe not. But I couldn't live with that, and I also knew I didn't want to live without him—not as long as I could do something about it.

I looked at the back of my hand, recalling how the symbol had glowed as it got close to that first turnstile. Then I stretched out my arm and spun in a slow circle, turning myself into a human compass. I stopped turning when the symbol began to glow just the tiniest bit brighter. "The next ride's this way."

I climbed out of the gully, and Maggie was quick to follow.

"Are you coming or not?" I asked Russ, and he reluctantly came along. For once *I* was the one pushing us full tilt toward the next ride.

6
Road Rage

We followed the growing glow on the backs of our hands until we came to a shiny black pond. Only it wasn't a pond. In fact, the surface was like smooth black glass. Objects moved across the obsidian face like huge, scurrying beetles—four feet long and waist high—but it was difficult to get a bead on what they were, because they weren't exactly . . . *there.* They kept shifting in and out of phase, appearing and disappearing, as if moving in and out of holes in some Swiss cheese dimension. It was Maggie who realized what they were.

"Bumper cars," she said.

As she said it I could swear I heard my brother's maniacal laugh amid the squeal of spinning tires.

Two bumper cars, one forest green, the other navy blue, appeared at the edge of our vision, and when we turned our focus toward them, they didn't dart off into oblivion. Instead, they remained empty and still. They were waiting for us.

"Only two?" said Maggie.

"Hey, you and me are a team," said Russ.

Maggie darted me a glance, but I looked away.

"I drive," Maggie said.

Russ guffawed, like it was the most ridiculous thing he had ever heard. "Not in this universe. I'll have you know I am the bumper car king."

"I'm still driving."

Russ grabbed her around the waist in his boyfriendly way. "Never mess with a guy and his wheels."

My ears flushed as I watched them. Maybe I was still mad at Russ from before. Maybe it was something new. Or maybe it was something that had always been there, filed neatly away. Well, it was time to do some refiling.

"I'll let you drive, Maggie. You can come with me," I said.

Russ was so surprised that he loosened his grip, and she eased out of it. He looked at me—not angry, but confused. "Why would she ride with you?" he asked.

"Because I'm not you," I told him. "Because I don't always have to drive."

He looked at me a moment more, considering it. "All right, I get your point." He smiled at Maggie. "I've been purged of the creep factor by Captain Courageous here." Then he took her hand gently. "You can drive."

She sort of accepted his sort-of apology, and all was well among the three of us again. Yet somehow this was not the resolution I had hoped for. I turned my attention to the bumper cars still waiting for us. I took the blue one, Russ and Maggie took the green. The car was so cramped, I had to bring my knees up at weird angles, and it was worse for Russ and Maggie, who had to sit toboggan style in a seat meant for much smaller people.

I looked out at another bumper car slipping in and out of existence, its rider screaming with some thrill we'd yet to experience.

"What do you think they see?" I asked, mainly to myself, but Maggie answered.

"I'll bet it's not stop signs."

There was a spark in her eye that reminded me of the spinning lights I saw in my brother's eyes when he lay unconscious. It gave me the vein chills, if you know what I mean.

This place is going to get her, I thought. *Maybe not on this ride, but on the next or the one after that.* I shook the thought away by flooring the accelerator.

The little wheels of the car spun, and I fishtailed. The pole rising from the rear of the car wiggled, extending upward. The electrical contact at its tip touched nothing but empty air.

As I accelerated the world began to change.

The sky was the first thing I noticed, how it went from angry red to tomato orange, like it was on fire. I looked at my watch in fear. Was this the light of sunrise? But the skies here had no bearing on time in the real world. According to my watch, it was only three in the morning.

The car began to change around me. At first I thought I was shrinking; but no—it was the steering wheel growing larger, it was the cramped leg space extending as well. The windshield and the dashboard spread out—everything was stretching like rubber. And in an instant

I knew I was no longer in a bumper car. I was driving something much, much bigger. Something old. Vintage, you might call it. See, I know my old cars. I had a collection of models on the shelves of my room. Pierce Arrows. Ford Hi-Boys. Sleek old cars with long silver grills: Beautiful machines, from the 1920s and '30s, when automobiles were both monstrous and sexy at the same time. But the vehicle I was driving now, well, it was a little more boxy than the other cars riding around me.

It was a Volvo.

I was in a 1931 Volvo, speeding down narrow cobblestone streets lined by brown-bricked buildings and old-fashioned billboards. In the blazing night sky above, a sliver of a moon hung on its side like a half-closed eyelid, and the bricks around me echoed a distant sound that I first took to be thunder. Then I realized it wasn't thunder at all. It was machine-gun fire. Now I knew what city this was supposed to be. This was Chicago, in the bad ol' days. This bumper car ride was a demolition derby in the middle of a gangster war.

"Clutch!" I heard Russ scream.

I looked over to see him and Maggie take out a fire hydrant as they turned down a side street. The hydrant became a geyser, and they disappeared down the street, part of their bumper trailing behind them. There were no road rules here, no order. Every car was a weapon.

Wham!

As if my thoughts weren't scrambled enough, I was rear-ended by a curly-haired twelve-year-old with teeth too long for his face and a crooked sneer. You know how your mom told you if you kept making an ugly face, it'd stay that way? Well, this kid's face did.

"You snooze, you bruise," he said, and took off down another street.

My neck hurt from the collision. I wanted more than anything to go after him and to nail his apple green Willys Coupe, all shiny and new. In that moment I had enough road rage to flatten a hundred sneering snots in their lousy little cars.

Lose yourself in it, an inner voice told me. *Floor that accelerator and ram someone. Anyone. Do it for all the times that someone hurt you and you couldn't do a thing about it. Make someone pay.* Sometimes it's like people leave their brain in the trunk before they get behind the wheel of a car, and that's exactly what was happening here. That's what this ride was all about.

I could listen to that voice, I knew I could. That would be the easy thing to do. Whether that voice was in my head or was *put* in my head, it didn't really matter, did it? The temptation was so overpowering. It was as irresistible as a summertime thirst, and I felt I'd do anything to quench it. Then I thought about Quinn, and that kept me from giving myself over to the ride. I was certain that he had already given himself over to the rides, which meant that I couldn't. I was the rational, sensible one. The balanced one. So I floored the accelerator, not at someone's bumper, but in search of Quinn. I was determined to find him, shake some sense into him, and drag him back home. I had one hand on the wheel.

It wasn't my normal ten-and-two position, but right then I didn't care.

I will not be caught up in this, I told myself. *I will drive, but I won't ride.*

I turned the wheel sharply to avoid being nailed by some other demolition derby driver bent on turning my car into scrap metal. I was a good driver. I was a safe driver. So what if this wasn't exactly a course in driver's ed? I'd make it through, and I wouldn't let myself be hit again.

Find your way to another ride. Cassandra's words echoed in my mind. Survive this and then find the next ride. Yes, find the next ride. . . . But first find Quinn.

I came to a major intersection, and that's where I finally saw him. Quinn was driving a blue Ford Hi-Boy, a freaky-looking thing with a grimace of a grill, as rude as he was. He whooped like a cowboy in a rodeo, his wheels screeching as he took off down another street, never even seeing me.

"*Quinn!*" But he was already gone.

I didn't see the car that hit me until it was too late. These old cars didn't have crumple zones—they didn't even have seat belts. I was broadsided from the right, but my backend took most of the blow; a single, sickening crunch, and my shoulder hit the side window. My car spun out, and when I came to a halt, I was facing the other car, which lay beached over a bus stop bench. The rider was a girl, about a year younger than me—probably not even old enough to drive.

"I'll get you, you stinking lousy . . ." She was practically frothing at the mouth, all the anger of her life funneled into this moment. Her forehead bled from the crash, but she didn't care about that. She tried to maneuver her car off the bench, but she couldn't.

"Oh, man, you're dust," she yelled. "I swear I'll get you!"

Road rage consumed her like a fungus, and yet this girl was enjoying it. This was an amusement park, all right. I suppose everything, even anger, can be worked into amusement. Knowing that helped me resist the urge to let it happen to me. Had Maggie and Russ given in to the rage? Had they joined the rampage of crashing cars? I didn't even know if I'd be able to find them again.

Closer than the distant screeches of tires, I heard the sound of an idling car. It was a deep, low rumble, more like a growl. Down the street was a tomato orange car with whitewall tires and dark windows. It was different from the other cars: longer, sleeker, and its sheen was the same fiery color of the sky. The angry girl in the beached car took one look at it and bailed, forgetting me and running for her life.

As the orange car slowly rolled forward, picking up speed, it was as if its tires barely touched the road. Weightless. Graceful. The car continued to accelerate to where my Volvo straddled the curb. The driver's side window rolled down, and a gray nozzle poked out.

I hurled my car into gear and floored the accelerator. My car seemed about to stall, but the gear grabbed and I lurched forward. Not fast enough. The orange car glided past, and through the window, I saw the bulging, circular cartridge of one of those old-fashioned gangster machine guns. *Rat-a-tat-tat*—that's just what it sounded like, just like it did in those old movies. I ducked as the blasts ripped up the side of my car and shattered my windows. I was just low enough to avoid getting hit.

This place isn't real, I told myself. *These bullets can't be real.*

And again, I wondered what would happen to me if I died on the ride.

The wreck I saw in the street ahead gave me my answer. It was the apple-green wreck of the obnoxious kid's car—the one who had nailed me when I first entered the ride. His car was upside down and burning. I didn't see him inside, but there was a billboard on the brick wall above the wreck. It was a Coca-Cola ad featuring the painted face of a kid holding a glass bottle of pop. It was the same kid who had been driving the car, and although his mouth smiled in the poster, his eyes stared out fixed in eternal horror above a caption that read: COKE! THE PAUSE THAT REFRESHES! If eyes could scream, the sound would have been bloodcurdling.

As I looked at the many billboards and advertisements plastered around the narrow maze of streets, every face on them had that same fixed expression. This was all that was left of the riders who hadn't survived the bumper cars.

The orange car had circled around and was coming back toward me, gliding in that weightless way. Time seemed to slow down, and I knew that if I didn't move soon, I'd wind up staring out of a toothpaste ad or something, with my own locked-jaw grin and shrieking eyes. I tried to open the door and jump out of the car, but the handle broke off in my hand, and when I turned to see what options I had, I realized it was too late. The orange car was already gliding past. I was about to hurl myself to the floorboards again, but all at once I was hit by a searing blast of déjà vu, as deadly as gunfire. For an instant I was not there. For an instant I was somewhere else.

Seven years old. The smell of bubble gum in the air. Landscape flying past a window . . . then a sports car, shiny tomato orange. The face in the car is a blur of shadows. But the eyes—they're in clear focus. Eyes as blue as glacier ice or a gas flame. I see them for an instant, through a school bus window. Then the orange car speeds up. It pulls in front of us, cutting us off. The bus driver spins the wheel, losing control and—

And I was back in the twisted mockery of old Chicago. The vision was gone, and although I didn't quite know where it had come from or what it meant, I knew it had unlocked a door somewhere deep inside me. It was a door that could come swinging open at any time, and, not knowing what was behind it, I wasn't so sure I liked it unlocked.

The orange car was gone. I climbed out through the broken window of my car and slipped away down an alley so narrow that I had to walk sideways. The alley opened into another street and up ahead there was a little tavern, its neon sign flickering red. A wave intersecting a spiral. The ride symbol. And as I looked at the symbol on the back of my hand, it began to glow. I slowly approached the tavern and pushed open the door.

A bell jingled, and as I let the door close behind me the dangerous sounds of the city became distant, like a low rumble of thunder—far enough away to know you were safe, but close enough to keep you on edge.

The place smelled of spilled beer and polished wood. It was deserted except for the bartender, who wiped down the bar with a rag.

"Hello, Blake," he said, with a broad smile. "Rough night out there?"

"How come you know my name?"

The smile never left his face. "I know all my customers."

I looked the place over, peering under tables, behind the bar, but I couldn't find a turnstile.

"Can I help you find something, sir?"

It seemed bizarre to me, this middle-aged man calling me "sir." I didn't feel like a sir. "I'm looking for the next ride."

"A ride?" He put down his rag, then pulled out an old-fashioned black telephone, with a circular dial, and left it on the counter. "If it's a ride you need, I could call you a taxi. But around here, I can't vouch for the drivers."

Out of curiosity, I picked up the receiver, wondering if it actually reached out of this place, like some landline to sanity. Instead of a dial tone, all I heard in the receiver was calliope music. I hung up quickly.

"Never mind."

The bartender pulled out a glass and deftly filled it

with what appeared at first to be beer. Then he poured in some of that red cherry-flavored stuff—grenadine, I think it's called   and topped it off with a cherry. He slid it down the bar toward me, not spilling a single drop.

"Compliments of the lady," he said, and nodded toward a tall-backed booth deep in the recesses of the pub.

I tasted my drink. Ginger ale and cherry syrup. A Shirley Temple. It was the kind of drink served to little kids too young to be humiliated by it.

I walked deeper into the bar to see what I had already suspected. The girl in the booth was Cassandra. She wore a flowing orange gown and a wide-brimmed hat, looking like something right out of a painting. Her copper hair flowed over her shoulders in a perfect fall. Smooth attitude poured from her like a scent. All the wires of everything I was feeling suddenly crossed at the sight of her, and I was at a loss.

"Was that you in the orange car, trying to kill me?"

"Do you want it to be?"

If I had chased her and cornered her, I might have acted differently. I might have demanded more answers right away, pushing until I got them. But she wasn't cornered. I didn't think she could be cornered in any situation. *She just tried to kill you!* I reminded myself, but the way she was looking at me now defused all my defenses. It was the same way she'd looked at me back at the ball-toss booth. As if she was drawn to me. As if she was somehow intrigued by me.

Who do you think you are? I said to myself. *Look at you,*

*standing here with your zits and your Shirley Temple. You
look like an idiot, and she knows it.*

Well, I didn't have to be. I wouldn't be.

I suavely slipped into the booth, pretending it didn't
hurt when I smashed my knee on the way in. "Thanks
for the Shirley Temple. But couldn't you at least have
gotten me a root beer?" I tried to match her mysterious
grin, but I had no idea whether I looked mysterious or
dorky. I tried to focus on her eyes, but whenever I did, I
couldn't hear a word she said.

Better get used to it, I thought. *There'll be Cassandras
everywhere once you get to college. If any girl there is ever
going to give you the time of day, you'd better work up some
major charisma. Fast.*

For an instant I thought of Maggie, with whom I
never had to work up anything but my own clunky self.
But seeing Cassandra right in front of me kind of blew
all other thoughts to smithereens.

"Enjoying yourself?" she asked.

I didn't care to answer that one, because my answer
wouldn't exactly be suave and charismatic. "It looks like
you sure are."

She shrugged. "I pass the time well."

"Is that what you call it—passing the time? Luring
people onto rides and watching them die?"

"They don't die," she said. "Not exactly."

"Exactly what happens to them, then?"

"You're in no position to ask questions."

"I'm asking anyway."

She considered that, then said, "If you lose your life

on a ride, the park just . . . absorbs you. Simple as that."
She stirred her drink, then touched the tip of my nose
with her straw. "There are worse things."

I didn't know if I was more taken or terrified by her.
"Who *are* you?" I finally asked.

She looked into me with those strange icy-hot eyes.
"Who am I? The sum of your dreams; the thrills you
refuse to grasp; the unknown you fear."

"Gee, thanks for the haiku, but a picture ID would
have been enough."

She wrinkled her nose, annoyed that I was no longer
falling for the mysterious-woman act. Score one for me.

She sighed, looking down into her drink. "If this
amusement park were flesh, then you could say I'm its
soul."

I grinned in spite of myself. "The spirit of adventure."

Then her expression darkened. "Yes. . . . And I'm
very, very bored."

I didn't like the sound of that. I felt a certain pressure
in my back that radiated outward, making my fingers
grow warm. An adrenaline rush. The kind that takes
hold when some primal part of you senses danger.

Suddenly Cassandra grabbed my hand. "Is that fear
you're feeling?"

I pulled my hand back. "It's none of your business
what I'm feeling."

She gave me an abrupt glare, as if I had slapped her,
but like all of her expressions, it quickly changed. She
was seductive and mysterious once more, but at least now
some of her mysteries had been exposed. "I shouldn't be

keeping you," she said. "After all, you've got five more rides to get through."

"Or else what?"

She smiled. "Sammy can answer that one for you." She turned to the bartender, who was still endlessly wiping down the dry, clean bar. "Sammy?"

"Yes, Miss Cassandra?"

"How long have you been with us?"

The smile drained from the bartender's face, and his eyes darted back and forth like it was a trick question.

"It's all right. You can answer," Cassandra said.

Sammy swallowed hard. "Of course, I'd be guessing . . . but I'd say about thirty years now. I was fifteen then. I was on my third ride when I got caught."

"Caught?"

"You know . . . dawn," said Sammy.

"The sun rises, and we close our gates," Cassandra said. "If you're not out of the park by dawn, then you stay."

I finally got the picture. Die on the ride and you're part of the scenery. Get caught alive and you're a slave of the park.

"There," said Cassandra. "Consider that incentive to play hard."

"It's not all that bad here," Sammy said, nervously wringing his hands. "I'd rather be here than in The Works, that's for sure."

"The Works? What's that?"

But Sammy looked down, refusing to say another word about it. Instead, he took up his role as bartender again. "Can I get anything more for you, sir?"

"I'm sure Blake must be hungry. Why don't you bring him the blue plate special?"

"Coming right up." Sammy disappeared into a small kitchen void of any chef.

I finished my stupid Shirley Temple, crunching the ice and gnawing at the cherry stem as I thought of my possible fates. Which was worse? Scenery or slavery?

Cassandra studied me. "You're not like the others who come here," she said. "You really don't want to ride."

That much was true. It seemed everyone else here—all the other invitees—couldn't wait to be a part of the thrills and chills.

"I guess you invited the wrong guy."

Suddenly a plate covered with a silver dome was deposited in front of me with a clatter.

"Here you are, sir. The blue plate special." Sammy returned to the bar, and the instant he was gone, Cassandra leaned forward and whispered with the kind of hushed intensity reserved for the most important of secrets.

"You're not here by mistake or by accident. I wanted you here tonight. You more than anyone."

Hearing that sucked the breath right out of me. I began to feel light-headed. "But . . . why would you want *me*?"

"Enjoy your meal." She stood up and sauntered casually away. She pulled open the door, setting off a jingle of bells and letting in the awful sounds of crashing cars.

After she was gone, I could still feel the residue of her presence—both her malevolence and her allure. I was attracted and repelled at the same time.

I wanted you here tonight, she had said. *You more than anyone.*

It stunned me to think I was singled out. Me, who never looked for attention the way Quinn did. Did she know I would never have come here if my brother hadn't stolen the invitation and come here first? Or was luring my brother here all part of her plan? If Cassandra was the soul of this place, that meant the amusement park was alive, and it wanted me—specifically wanted *me*.

I closed my eyes and took a few moments to try to defragment my brain. Then I opened my eyes again, and looked down to the platter in front of me, wondering exactly what the blue plate special might be. I hoped it wasn't the broiled head of anyone I knew. A puff of steam escaped as I pulled away the dome, revealing that the plate was, indeed, blue. But there was nothing on it. Nothing but two words written across the plate:

NO

ᗡ⅃OH

I had no idea what that meant until I realized that the *D* was printed backward. I rotated the plate around.

HOLD

ON

★ ★ ★

The glowing ride symbol on my hand went dark, as if it had been scanned by the blue plate special, and then the booth suddenly spun like one of those haunted-house bookshelves that leads to a tunnel. The booth was revolving into the wall like . . .

Like a turnstile!

The entire booth turned 180 degrees, closing out the restaurant and leaving me sitting on the other side of the wall.

7

Big Blue Mother

I was in a warehouse, and I was alone. That was what struck me instantly—being alone. Through everything, I'd been surrounded by others: wild riders on the carousel, frenzied drivers on the streets of Chicago. But the revolving tavern booth deposited me in a lonely warehouse graveyard of battered cars and piles of rusted automotive parts, the waste products of my last ride.

The warehouse was huge, at least fifty feet high, with great stone pillars holding up the ceiling and long windows made of hundreds of smaller panes of glass. I could see nothing through those panes, only the sky, casting a cage of shadows on the ground. Yet beyond the windows the sky was changing. The shades of orange spoiled to amber and a sickly yellow, like the skin around an old bruise. If the booth was a turnstile, then I was already on the approach to a new ride, but I didn't yet know what it was.

There was a sound now. It was the *swish-swish-swish* of something slicing back and forth like a pendulum. As I moved around a pile of junk I saw its shadow, huge and ominous, as it rose and fell. Only now did I hear the screams each time it fell. Finally it came into view, a thing strangely out of place within this warehouse.

It was the swinging boat—the one we had seen when we first entered the park. It was in the form of a three-masted schooner, and it hung from a single axle supported on both sides. It swung forward and back, forward and back, with a rhythm that was both hypnotic and nauseating. This was what the ride looked like from the outside. But from the *inside*, what would it be? I didn't have to wait long to find out. The warehouse had sprung a leak. As I leaned against a pillar water ran over my hand. I looked down to see myself standing in a puddle that kept growing deeper, because the water wasn't just dribbling down the pillar now, it was pouring. Beyond the windows of the huge warehouse an ocean was rising.

I wanted to keep it out. I wanted to keep *everything* out: the fact that Cassandra had set her sights on me; that I'd lost Maggie and Russ; that my brother kept spiraling deeper into the rides. . . .

The windows began to explode inward with the force of the ocean, spilling into the warehouse. A white-water wave rolled behind me, and in front of me was the swinging boat. All my hope rested in the sanctuary of that vessel.

The water that just a moment ago was at my ankles now rose past my knees, and I could hear the wave roaring behind me. The wave hit me, washing me off my feet. I reached up and managed to hook my arm around one of the support struts holding up the ride. With the icy water at my chest now, the boat crashed down, taking me under. It dragged me along its rough hull, pressing the air out of my lungs, bruising me, and scraping me across barnacles until I couldn't tell up from down.

When I finally surfaced, the support struts were gone, the warehouse was gone, but the boat and the waves were still there, much bigger than before. If swimming were not my sport, I would have drowned by now, but even so, it took all my strength to keep my head above the waves. The boat—now a life-size schooner—lurched forward and crashed down over the waves with a motion not all that different from when it had been attached to a greasy axle. Up above, a storm raged in a strange sky the color of dark mustard.

A rope dangled from the bow, and as the bow plunged I grabbed that rope with both hands, wrapped it around my right leg, and clamped it tightly to the instep of my left foot—just like they taught us in gym class. As the boat rose with the next swell I was lifted out of the water.

Maybe it was adrenaline, or maybe I just weighed less in this weird world, but I was able to pull myself up hand over hand. I clasped the rope to keep from being hurled off each time the ship hit the bottom of a swell, and I used the upward energy to climb faster each time it peaked, until I finally spilled over onto the deck. My lungs were half full of water and my hands were red and raw, but I was still alive and riding.

The boat pitched beneath me with a regular stomach-churning rhythm, a feeling that just grew worse with each wave. And with each of those waves, the old schooner peaked and I heard voices screaming up above. I looked up to see kids—dozens of them—high above the deck, clinging to the web of ropes that hung from the masts and beams. *Ratlines,* that's the word. They swung from the ratlines. Some of them swung from the beams themselves, and others gripped the tattered fragments of the shredding sails.

You know how when you were little, your dad would throw you up and down in the pool until you were giddy with laughter? I know, because it's one of the few memories I have of my father. Well, that's how these riders were. Giddy. But when they fell from their high perches, doing cartwheels into the sea, nobody was there to catch them.

The schooner crested another wave, the bow rising and plunging again. Up above, the riders squealed with joy. Icy water rolled across the deck, washing me up against the foremast. Then a hairy hand grabbed me by the shirt and pulled me to my feet.

"What nature a' fool be ya, boy? Rollin' around on the deck when there's work t'be done!" The man's face was covered by a heavy beard. His voice, somehow familiar, was masked in an accent that was almost but not quite like a pirate's.

With his hand still on the collar of my shirt, he hauled me to the railing. "Fix your eyes on the sea and nothing else," he told me.

Then I caught something huge out of the corner of my eye, almost the color of the waves. I turned in time to see the tail end of a barnacle-encrusted whale larger than the ship. I was awestruck by the sight.

"Aye, breach your last to the sun!" the bearded man shouted to the whale. "The hour and thy harpoon are at hand!" The great whale's fluke cut a wide arc and slipped back into the water.

Oh no. By now I had a good idea what this ride was.

A huge wave caught us, the wake of the whale's breach. It almost washed me away from the railing, but I held on tight. Above us another unfortunate rider plunged into the frothing sea.

"Drive, drive in your nails, o ye waves. To their uttermost heads, drive them in!" the bearded captain raved.

I still had the feeling that this ride was neither random nor the manifestation of someone else's mind. Just as with the carousel, I had a powerful sense that Cassandra had reached inside my mind to create this ride, but I couldn't figure out why she had chosen *this.* I never even liked *Moby Dick.*

"Ready to lower the boats!" Captain Ahab shouted. "Today we take the great blue whale!"

"Uh . . . don't you mean great *white* whale?"

"Nay, boy. The blue whale be our quarry on this cursed voyage. The greatest creature on land or sea. She has no teeth to tear a man to shreds like the white whale of which you speak, but she is awesome and daunting prey, nonetheless."

A loud hiss, and I turned to see the great blue whale surface again, spouting spray from its blowhole. Its huge eye was somehow familiar. Its shape, its color. It wasn't the strange blue of Cassandra's eyes; this eye was speckled brown. I knew if I had time to think, I'd be able to place where I'd seen such an eye before.

I watched as the whale opened its tremendous mouth and drew in water. I could see tiny shrimp writhing against the bony lattice in its mouth.

"See how she opens her mouth to filter life from the sea!" said the captain. "I'd hate to be a krill caught in *her* baleen."

And all at once it clicked.

Krill . . . Baleen . . . This *was* a thought tugged right out of my mind. I took a good, hard look at the maniacal captain, trying to pick the shape of his face out from beneath his heavy beard. *"Carl?"* Then I looked to the sea, at the submerging whale. *"Mom?"*

Carl put his hand on my shoulder. "Keep your wits about you, boy."

"You can't really be here, right? You're just some fig-ment of my imagination. Just a part of the ride, right? *Right?*"

He just ignored me, looking out to sea for a sign of the whale. "I struck my first whale as a boy harpooner of eighteen. But this one here is the great prize, and beyond her there will be no other. Will you help me, boy?"

"No! I mean, yes! I mean, I don't know!"

The bow crashed down again, and as we rose and crested the next swell I saw a reef off the starboard bow—jagged granite rocks that thrust up through the churning sea like teeth. I could see bits and pieces of other ships in the crevices of the stone monoliths.

"Follow her into the reef!" shouted mad Captain Carl. A sailor at the helm wildly spun the tiller, and the ship turned toward the rocks.

Up above me the riders still wailed with joy as they swung from the ratlines. One of those voices sounded familiar. It was a shrill whoop that I'd heard so many times, I could place it a mile away. I looked up. In a flash of lightning across the mottled yellow sky, I saw Quinn clinging to the highest of the ratlines, right beneath the crow's nest. He screamed in defiance of the crashing waves, daring them to shake him loose.

Fighting the violent pitching of the ship, I climbed the ratlines toward him. I was almost thrown from the ropes, but I held on with what little strength my fingers had left, until I finally reached him high up where the ratlines met the mast.

"Toward thee I roll," the mad captain shouted at the whale with my mother's eyes. "To the last, I grapple with thee!"

"Quinn!" I could barely hear my own voice over the thunder and wind. I was right next to him now, and still he didn't know I was there. He just kept whooping as the boat pitched up and down, the motion intensified by the height of the mast. He was oblivious to Carl, our mother the whale, or anything else outside the rush of the ride.

"Quinn!"

Finally he turned to me, blinking like he had just come out of a trance. His eyes were wide and wet from the cold wind. *"Blake?* When did *you* get here?"

There was a deafening blast, and a surge of electricity

made my arm hairs tingle. A kid on the foremast had been struck by lightning. His smoking body tumbled limply, missing the deck and plunging into the sea. Then I caught sight of one of the passing spires of rock. Part of the stone seemed to melt away, forming a face. In fact, all over the reef, I could swear I saw giant faces in the stone, the wailing mouths and hopeless eyes of those whose lives were given to the ride.

Lightning sparked in the sky again as I realized we were clinging to the highest point of the boat. Then I looked at Quinn's moronically metallic face. Dangling chains and rings—all perfect electrical conductors.

"You're a lightning rod! You've got to get down from here!"

"No way!" He returned his gaze forward. "I'm not letting you spoil this! It's the best ride yet!"

With Quinn, action always speaks louder than words, so I tugged him from the rope net, and we both fell, rolling down the rough ratlines, bouncing painfully off the boom, and landing hard on the deck.

"This ship's going down!" I told him, ignoring my aches from the fall.

"How do *you* know? You don't know everything."

"I know the story. One way or another, this ship is going down." I looked around for something—anything that would give us an out. Then I caught sight of a strange, unearthly light escaping around the edges of a closed hatch. I knelt down and pulled at the hatch with all my strength. Finally it popped open.

The light within was too bright. My eyes fought to

adjust, and for an instant I got the briefest glimpse of bright chrome gears turning. They were pieces of some colossal gear-work that couldn't possibly fit in the hold of a ship. This hatch was a doorway to another place entirely!

The Works, I thought. *It must be The Works!*

Beyond that hatch was the mechanism that ran every ride. But before I could get a better look, crazy Captain Carl slammed it shut with his foot.

"Nobody goes below!"

Just then the whale breached right beside the ship.

"Was that a whale?" Quinn asked, clueless as ever. "What's up with *that*?"

As the whale with my mother's eyes came down, the force of its wake threw the ship against the rocks with a shattering of wood.

"Blast ye!" yelled that strange blending of Captain Ahab and my mother's fiancé. He threw his fists to the sky. "The madness, the frenzy, the boiling blood, and the smoking brow!"

"That's it, we're outta here." I pushed Quinn to the railing. "Jump. Now!"

"Are we gonna ride the whale? Is that part of the ride?"

"Just jump!" I practically hurled him over the side, and followed right behind. I hit the icy water. Then, for an instant, I felt something huge and rough brush right past me. I fought my way to the surface, breaking through into the noise of the storm.

Quinn sputtered beside me. He wasn't as strong a

swimmer as I was, so I tried to help him, but he wouldn't let me. He kicked me away and began swimming toward the rocks. I turned back to see the ship, twenty yards away now . . . and then a blue gray wall rose in front of me. The whale breached again, but this time it came down right on the ship. Riders were thrown from the rat-lines. The ship cracked in half, and in a few moments both whale and ship were gone into the darkness of the churning sea.

A wave hurled me onto the rocks, where brand-new faces were appearing. I tried not to look directly at them; I was afraid I'd be too horrified to move if I did.

When I turned to look for Quinn, he was scrambling away over the rocks.

"No!" I grabbed him by his collar as we reached a wide plateau. I was so mad, I would have grabbed him by his nose ring if I could get my finger through it. "You're not getting away from me again!"

"Why did you have to come?" he yelled. "You ruined everything! You made me miss the best part of the ride!"

"Best part? What, are you out of your mind? If you went down with that ship, you wouldn't be coming back up."

And then Quinn looked me dead in the eyes. *"Who says I wanted to?"*

If my temper was a burning fuse, that pinched it right off. My head reeled from what he said. From what he *meant.*

"Who says I want to do anything but finish the ride?"

I took a deep breath, and another, as I stared at him.

The sound of the ocean raged behind us, but right now I could hear only him. "What are you saying, Quinn?"

"You came here to save me from this place, didn't you? But who said I want to be saved this time?"

I opened my mouth to speak, but all my words had been robbed from me. What could I say to him? What could I say to my brother, who came here not just for the thrills, but for something else? As much as I didn't want to face it, I had to now. Somehow he knew where these rides would end. He knew that once he crossed through the gates, he wasn't coming back. He knew, and still he had come.

"What's out there for me, huh?" Quinn's eyes flowed with tears, and those tears flowed with a dozen different emotions. "What's ever been out there for me? When I'm at home, it's like I'm . . . it's like I'm empty on the inside. You don't know what that's like."

They say that before someone takes their own life, there's always a cry for help. Sometimes it's loud, and you have to be seriously deaf not to hear it. Sometimes it's just a word or a look, like the look Quinn was giving me right now. I might have been deaf to it before, but that look screamed louder than anything now. I had no skill in talking someone in from the edge, and that space between us was still a whole universe wide.

"Quinn . . ."

"It's not your job to save me, so give it up, huh? Please . . . just give it up."

"It's not a job," I told him. "It's something I've got to do. Something that I *need* to do."

"But why?" Quinn asked. "Is it because of what happened on the school bus?"

I looked away from him. "Mom shouldn't have told you about that."

"She didn't. I just heard." Quinn hesitated for a moment. I thought he might take a step closer. "Is it true that you're the only one who survived?"

I took a deep breath. "Let's go home, and we can talk about it there."

Quinn thought about it and shrugged sadly. "Some people are survivors. Some aren't."

"And how do you know you're not? Just because things stink now and you feel empty inside, it doesn't mean you'll feel that way next week, or next month, or next year!"

"That's just words!" Quinn said, getting more frustrated. "Hell, I don't have the patience to play a game of Scrabble, and I'm supposed to hang on your words for months and years?" He looked down. His shoulders dropped. I could see into *his* works now—the angry pistons, the overheated gears, and that pit inside of him. He kept it so well hidden back home with attitude, but here, it was bare and bottomless. A wave crashed behind me. I could feel it vibrating up my legs and into my joints.

"Sometimes I just want to disappear . . . y'know?" Quinn looked around at the tortured faces in the rocks around us. "Can you think of a better place to do it?"

"I'll never let you disappear, Quinn."

I locked on his teary eyes and imagined that I had tractor beams in mine, that my gaze would somehow pull him in. "Come on," I told him. "We'll ride out of this place together."

He took one step closer, then another. I reached my hand toward him, he reached out his—

And then the symbol on the back of his hand began to glow.

From deep in a cave behind him came the distant, hollow cries of other kids in the middle of one last thrill.

Quinn backed away from me. "I kinda got used to riding alone." Then he turned toward the cave.

I was losing him again. I didn't know what else to say that would get through to him, so I leveled the truth at him with both barrels.

"You're lying in a coma in the hospital!" I shouted. "They carted you away in an ambulance, and that's where you are!"

It was harsh, like waking a sleepwalker; but it stopped him in his tracks. "At least that's what Mom thinks," I said, trying to ease the blow.

Without even turning to look at me, he said, "Maybe it's best she thinks that." Then he leaped into the gaping mouth of the cave and the darkness swallowed him.

I sat on the rocks among the silent stone faces, with no desire to go on. I could have leaped into the darkness after Quinn, following him to his next ride, but what was the point? How do you help someone who refuses to be helped? Was I supposed to knock him unconscious and drag him out of here? He was already unconscious.

There was a flash of yellow light. Far off in the ocean

a new ship appeared out of nowhere, sailing closer. This time it was a Spanish galleon—somebody else's nightmare. The swinging boat sailed again, filled with a whole new batch of riders headed toward some different adventure but the same fate.

"You're not playing," I heard Cassandra say. She sat on a rock just a few feet away, dressed in a bright yellow silk gown, a garland of flowers and shells woven into her hair. She looked like something from mythology: a beautiful siren, luring sailors to their death. "You made it through this ride. Now move to the next." Although her voice was restrained, her words still sounded like an order.

"Why are you following *me*? You have a park full of riders, happy to hand their lives to you. Leave me alone! Like you said, I didn't come for your rides."

"No, you came for your brother. But he'll be lost, just like everyone else."

Her words echoed around inside my head a few times before catching on some receptive brain tissue. "What do you mean, 'like everyone else'?"

She stood and came closer. "Seven rides, each one harder than the last. Think about it, Blake."

"Are you saying that *no one's* ever made it through all seven rides?"

She turned with only mild interest at the approaching galleon. "They're lured by the thrill, and soon there's nothing else. Even though there's a way out of every single ride, they rarely find it, or even look for it. They let the thrill consume them. In the end either the ride takes them or they get caught at dawn. Either way, they never leave."

In the sea beside us the galleon careened along the reef until something huge, green, and reptilian rose from the depths to grab its masts, pulling it over on its side, flinging riders into the sea. If there was a way out of every ride, like she said, these riders had missed their chance. The creature pulled riders from the ratlines with its clawed hands, shoving them into its tooth-filled mouth. Rocks eroded into astonished faces. *Here be serpents,* the medieval maps all warned.

"How can you do this to people? Lure them here, only to destroy them?"

"It's a matter of balance," she said coolly.

"What are you talking about?"

She laughed at me. "You don't think this park grows out of nowhere, do you? It has to be built, attraction by attraction, on the spirits of those who visit."

A roar from the serpent, and the last of the galleon was taken under the waves. So if this park was a living thing, a creature existing in the rift between dreams and the real world, then the riders—*all* the riders—were merely prey; and I had been watching the creature feed.

Cassandra took another step forward. "You're afraid! Tell me about your fear, Blake."

"I won't tell you anything!"

"Please. I want to know what it's like. I want to know fear."

As I forced myself to look at her I could see she wasn't just toying with me. She wanted to know. She wanted to *feel* what I felt. She studied me. I could feel her pulling at my thoughts, trying to get ahold of my feelings, and failing. She didn't know fear. How could she, when the danger was always someone else's?

This time it was I who took a step closer to her. I've always suspected that my life—maybe everyone's life—is like an hourglass, in which the past and the future converge on a single point in time, that narrow channel where the sands pass. A single event that defines who you are. Until now I had thought that the bus accident was that event for me; yet here was a moment not of blind helplessness, but of decision. Everything could rest in the balance of the choice I now made.

Without daring to think about it, I reached for Cassandra, pulled her toward me, and kissed her. It wasn't a kiss of passion—well, maybe just a little. But more than anything it was a kiss of defiance. A fear-conquering, do-or-die act of affirmation. Of determination.

In the instant that our lips touched, I felt what she truly was. Intense heat encased in intense cold. Two opposing extremes. But I was neither seared nor frozen by her.

I will not die in this place. I refuse to be plunged from existence. I will no longer be at the mercy of these rides. They will be at my *mercy. I will make it through all seven, and I will get out. I will be the one.*

I pulled away, my fear gone. The strength of my resolve was like an engine inside of me.

Cassandra smiled. She knew what that kiss meant every bit as much as I did.

"I accept your challenge," she said. "From this moment on, no more games. The next time you see me I'll be coming in for the kill."

Perhaps she couldn't sense my feelings, but I could sense hers. Excitement—perhaps for the first time. I was the ticket to her own private thrill ride.

Another flash of yellow light. In the distance a ship appeared again—this time a Viking ship. I imagined it was about to sail off the edge of the earth or something equally unpleasant.

"I'm making it out of here before dawn," I told Cassandra. "Me and anyone I can take with me."

Again that sultry grin. "Knock yourself out."

I turned my back on her and marched toward the wailing cave into which Quinn had hurled himself. But Cassandra took her first strike against me unexpectedly.

"You began riding young, didn't you, Blake?"

I didn't want to listen, but I couldn't keep myself from hearing. I couldn't keep her words from piercing my brain.

"And your bus never made it to school that day."

It was a shot in the back—not a shot to kill me, but one to disable me. Her words sliced through my defenses like a hot blade, and I could feel it searing deep inside me. Was I that vulnerable? I winced, feeling the blow almost like a physical pain, but I found that I could tolerate it without falling apart. I was finding a whole lot of things I could tolerate more than I thought I could.

Before me was a cave that appeared to have no bottom. An abyss of darkness. But somehow that unknown was less intimidating than it had been only a few moments before.

Three rides done. Four to go.

With my eyes open wide, I leaped into the cave.

8
Our Lady of Perpetual Reflection

The rides are different for everyone. I'm convinced of that now. I mean, sure, there are some we ride together. Either we find ourselves drawn to some common experience, or maybe we're pulled in by the people we care about. Our friends, our families can drag us onto coasters and Tilt-A-Whirls that are really meant for them. But in the end, no matter whose rides we find ourselves on, the experience is all our own.

Out of the blackness of the pit I had leaped into came a flash of green. I hit ground suddenly, a bruising belly flop on hard-packed earth. In the outside world I would have been killed, but here, there were other things to kill you besides the drop. Here, it only stung for a few moments.

With the wind knocked out of me, I took a few seconds to catch my breath before sitting up to take in my surroundings. I was on a wasteland—a cracked, blistered salt flat, void of life. Bleak desolation spread out in all directions like a place God had leveled for construction and then abandoned.

The sky was a flat pea green and made my skin look pallid and sickly. Only one structure stood on the endless salt flat. It was a mile or so ahead, shimmering like a mirage in the misty air. I ran toward it, not wanting to waste any more of my precious time. According to my watch, it was already three thirty in real time. That gave me only two and a half hours to make it through four more rides.

As I neared the structure in the distance I could see others like myself running toward the building from all directions. More riders gathering for their next ride. One of them bumped past me as if I weren't even there. He was in a trance. They were all like that. To these riders, the space between rides was just mental airspace, devoid of anything but the will to move through the next turnstile. I was different. Yes, I could feel the gravity of the ride pulling me toward it, but it didn't capture me the way it captured the others. *Why not?* I wondered. What was it about me that made me able to resist? What was it about me that made Cassandra see me as a worthy adversary?

The building resolved out of the mist. It was a cathedral. Notre Dame, to be exact. I knew from my poster of France. I recognized its two great spires on either side of a circular stained-glass window. Only in *this* Notre Dame, the stained-glass window was all red and leered like a single Cyclops eye. As for the stonework of the cathedral, it wasn't stone at all; it was reflective glass. A hall of mirrors.

Others kept pushing past me, the ride symbols on the backs of their hands glowing as they approached the turnstile.

A mirror maze, I thought. How bad could it be? Then I laughed at the stupidity of my own question. Trapped in a maze of mirrors for eternity? Shredded by bits of broken glass? Yeah, it could be pretty bad.

I wondered if Quinn had passed this way or if his path had taken him to another ride. Regardless, the only way now was forward through the glass doors of the crystalline Notre Dame Cathedral, so I ran my hand over the scanner and pushed myself through the turnstile, into the maze of mirrors.

I once got lost in the mall when I was really little. It was before I could read, before I knew left from right, and my mother's hand was the only thing that kept me safe from the big bad world. When you're scared like that, all the stores and all the turns begin to look the same. You truly believe in the pit of your little-kid mind that you're never going to be found. That's exactly how it felt to face the maze of mirrors.

The halls were narrow, the turns unpredictable, and the dead ends demoralizing. I kept winding my way down paths, swearing I could see the reflection of an exit, only to have to turn around and try again.

That wasn't even the worst part. The worst part was the clowns. I don't know if everyone saw them as clowns, but I sure did. Big floppy feet, a rim of ridiculous red hair—oh, and battle camouflage. These were commando clowns. It was a recurring nightmare I'd had ever since I was little. Don't ask.

But even worse than in my dreams, these clowns were

all armed with heavy artillery, and they fired huge mortar shells down the narrow glass corridors from bazookas on their shoulders. Those shells never shattered the glass, instead, they rebounded off, reflected like light, ricocheting in all directions until some poor slob got in the way and was blown to kingdom come. Never once did a mirror break from the explosions.

I crawled and rolled to keep out of their sight and out of the killing path of their weapons. Bones littered the ground of this awful place, crunching beneath me as I crawled. They were dry and blanched, like bones left under a hot desert sun. These were the kinds of bones you always saw on the ground in bad westerns, before the wagon train got attacked by Indians or the settlers had to start eating one another to stay alive. The thing was, these bones in the maze didn't resemble anything I knew about. It wasn't so much their size as their shape that was grotesque. I shuddered to think what kind of monsters might lie deeper in this mirror maze that could have given rise to such remains.

As I dodged and crawled through the reflective battle zone, I began to get an understanding of the mirrors themselves. Some appeared to be plain old fun-house mirrors, pulling and twisting your reflection into something barely recognizable. Other mirrors were far worse. When you looked in some of them, your reflection appeared exactly the same, but the way you *felt* about what you saw was warped and distorted. There was this one mirror that made me see myself as weak and cowardly and another that made me feel so overwhelmingly inadequate, I felt I'd shrivel into nothingness if I looked too long. Another mirror made me feel as if I were intensely stupid, and another magnified the fear in my soul so much, I was afraid I might scream and never stop. No mirrors in the real world had the ability to reach inside you the way these did. You could tell yourself that the mirrors were simply telling lies, but you'd be wrong. They took tiny truths, swelling them out of proportion—and the fact that there was a kernel of truth in what they reflected made the effect devastating. Now I realized that all the wails I'd been hearing far off in the maze weren't just from riders falling victim to the bozo brigade; they were the wails of riders torn apart by the twisted reflections of their own inner selves.

I did my best to keep from looking in any more mirrors, but it was harder than you might think. Once you started looking into those mirrors, it was next to impossible to look away. I guess we all can't help peeking at our own imperfections, just like we can't help scratching a scab that keeps itching. When those imperfections are pasted across your face like that, exaggerated and magnified, it's hard to find all those good thoughts you have about yourself. If you believe those distorted reflections too deeply, you'll never get out of the maze.

A mortar shell rocketed my way, and I hit the floor as it shot past, ricocheting deeper into the "fun" house. That's when I came face-to-face with a skull. I yelped in surprise. Like the other bones in this place, it was far from human. It was lopsided and gourd-shaped, with one eye socket the size of a baseball and the other the size of a marble. Its nasal cavity was as twisted as a snail shell, and its jaw was filled with mismatched teeth that would plague a dentist's darkest dreams. Not human. Not even close. There was a thigh bone, too—at least I think it was a thigh bone—in the shape of an *S*. I tried to imagine the creature that would have bones like this, but I couldn't fit it into my imagination. Turned out I didn't have to, because I suddenly heard a sickly, raspy breathing behind me.

One of those things had found me.

I turned to see it lumbering toward me. It was no larger than I was, but its ugliness made it seem immense. To say the thing was hideous did not do it justice. It was an awful mockery of life: ragged, protruding ears, one higher than the other; shoulders set in an uneven slouch, like a living landslide; and a spine hunched in a roller-coaster curve that made my back hurt just looking at it. It had one huge elephant eye, a tiny shrunken one, and its arms were shriveled like the limbs of a T-Rex, ending in stubby, clawlike fingers. Have you ever seen the figures Picasso painted? Well, this thing was like a Picasso from hell. If I had one of those clown's bazookas, I would have put it out of its misery right then and there.

It loped closer, and I took a healthy step away. "Back off, Quasimodo!"

It opened its swollen, crooked mouth and let loose a moan. Then it lunged for me, claws reaching for my throat. I swung the skull at it, hitting it on the shoulder, and ran, making turn after turn in the narrow corridors of mirrors, until I found myself at yet another dead end. I pivoted, thinking the creature was still behind me, but I'd lost it, for now.

I was still holding the misshapen skull—a good thing too, because if I had dropped it on the way, I would never have made the connection. Now I happened to look at the mirror in front of me. It was your standard distorting mirror, stretching and distending my image, but the reflection of the skull didn't quite look that way. In fact, the twisted skull, when reflected by the twisted mirror, was the perfect reflection of a *human* skull! I looked at the lopsided skull again and back at its perfect reflection. Then I reached out with my free hand and touched the surface of the mirror.

My hand passed through the glass as if there were no glass at all.

I could see my fingers on the other side of the mirror, and I almost screamed. They were short, stubby claws. I moved my fingers, feeling how my flesh had changed once they'd passed through the looking glass. I pulled my hand back quickly, and my fingers returned to normal, tingling from the change they had undergone when they had passed through.

Then I heard a sound behind me and turned to see the creature once more. It was breathing heavily, tears rolling down its stretched face, splashing onto its huge, bulging belly. It didn't chase me, but loped toward me cautiously, and I grimaced. *Does your face hurt?* the old joke goes. *Because it's killing me.*

The creature got closer and looked at me for a long time. Then it looked down at its bloated belly and said in a wet, slippery voice, "Do I look fat to you?"

My knees buckled. I almost fell through one of the distorting mirrors but kept enough of my balance to stay on the right side of the glass.

"*Maggie?* Is that you?"

And she sadly nodded her lopsided head.

"Crashed our bumper car," Maggie said as we crouched at the dead end, listening to the distant wails and explosions echoing in the maze. At first I couldn't understand her speech, filtered through that mess of a mouth. But after a while it was kind of like listening to Shakespeare: The more I listened, the more I could understand.

"Crashed our bumper car but couldn't stop. Had to get another car. Had to ride. Don't know why. Couldn't stop."

"It's all right," I told her. "I know what this place does to you. Tell me what happened next."

She drew a deep breath and rested for a moment. It was a real chore for her to speak with her tongue so thick and her jaw so misaligned. "Found a manhole cover. Ride symbol on it. Knew it was the next ride. Pried it open. Jumped in. Wound up here." Maggie reached up a distorted hand and wiped away a tear from her smaller eye.

"Where's Russ?" I asked her. "What happened to him?"

She shuddered. I could see that this was the hardest part for her, and I braced myself for the worst.

"Running through the mirrors. Both of us. I fell. I fell again, through the mirrors. One mirror, then another, then another. Couldn't find the first one. Kept trying, couldn't find it." Her voice got higher and harder to understand. Now her large, swollen eye began to drip heavy tears. "Russ saw me. He saw me, and he didn't help me. He saw me like this, and he ran. Couldn't look at me. He ran!"

After that her words dissolved into sobs, I reached out and took her in my arms as best I could.

"I won't run from you," I told her.

"You did!" she accused. "You did, you did, you did!"

"I didn't know it was you!"

But that didn't stop her tears. "Russ knew!" she wailed. "Russ knew, and he ran anyway."

"I'm not Russ!"

Slowly she began to calm down. Far off I heard another blast, and booted footsteps resounding through the maze, but I didn't care about all that right now. I know this is a strange thing to say, but I'd never felt closer to Maggie than I did at that moment.

I found myself leaning forward and kissing those swollen, sagging lips. It was the most repulsive thing I had ever done, yet it was the most wonderful. When I looked at her again, she'd stopped crying. She was still the same mess she'd been a moment before. I mean, it wasn't like the kiss had changed her from a frog into a princess, but something had changed in both of us in that weird little moment.

"I'll fix everything," I told her, promised her, swore to

her. There was a way out of every ride. Cassandra had said so herself. Not just for me, but for Maggie, too. And maybe . . . maybe even for Quinn.

"Listen," I told her, "this path was a dead end, but the next one might not be. We'll go together." I took her misshapen hand and held it tight. "I won't let you go." But she was not quite ready to believe me.

"I hate myself," she said, not wanting to look me in the eye. "I always have."

And maybe from somewhere deep down, she was telling the truth. I mean, I know I've hated myself from time to time. But the thing is, that feeling comes and it goes. Mostly it goes. But I figured Maggie had fallen through one of the distorting mirrors that took that tiny little feeling and made it so big that it buried everything else under it.

"Russ was right to run from me."

She must have fallen through the feel-sorry-for-yourself mirror, too. This situation was getting much too serious, so I looked at her stretched jaw. "C'mon, Maggie, why the long face?"

"Ha-ha." She hit me on the arm, but I just smiled back. I can't quite say I grew used to the distorted image she'd made of herself, but I'd stretched my own mind enough to accept it.

"Stop looking at me!" she said, hiding her face. "I'm terrible. I'm so ugly!"

And then I got an idea. It was either a really great idea or a really bad one, but I was willing to take my chances. I smiled at her. "You can say that again!"

She looked at me, uncertainly. "What?"

"You're not just butt ugly," I continued, "and you're not just coyote ugly—you're coyote butt ugly."

"Shut up!"

"You're so ugly, your driver's license doesn't have a picture. Instead, it just says, 'You don't wanna know.'"

"Stop it!" she yelled, but now she was laughing.

"You're so ugly that . . . you're so ugly that . . ." But I was fresh out of lame ugly jokes.

So *she* came up with one: "I'm so ugly, my face is registered as a lethal weapon."

I laughed, she laughed, and before long we were both caught up in one of those silly giggle fits where you can't even catch your breath. And it was great, because suddenly it didn't matter what she looked like. I could see gratitude in those mismatched eyes, and they were the same shade of green they'd always been. I could still see the girl I knew.

We wound around deeper into the maze, encountering dead end after dead end. I tried to keep track of every turn we took, but it was just too much. Every once in a while we encountered other mutated riders. Some were furious and waved their arms at us angrily. Others were terrified and ran away. Still others just sat there morosely, like orangutans at the zoo, resigned to their condition.

"If I can just figure out the combination of mirrors you passed through," I said to Maggie, "we could get you back to normal."

"I tried," she said. "I tried too many. I kept turning right, then left. Didn't do any good. Each one was worse."

And then something occurred to me. None of these mirrors were solid—not a single one—which meant that the mirrors weren't actually holding us in.

There were no walls holding us in!

I turned to face the mirror beside me. Could it be that easy? Of course it could. What better joke for Cassandra to pull than to make the answer so obvious, you looked right past it? You walked around it, changing direction again and again and again.

I looked at my reflection. One shoulder higher than the other, a nasty curved spine. I took a step toward the mirror, and Maggie squeezed my hand hard.

"No! Don't!"

"Trust me," I told her. There was no reason she should; I knew no more than she did. But she took a deep breath, and together we stepped forward, through the mirror.

I felt the change like an electric shock as I merged with my reflection, becoming what I saw. I could feel the distortion inside me—the sickening swelling of organs and the shifting of bones—but I refused to panic. I held tightly to Maggie's hand. I didn't turn around, I didn't turn left or right, getting confused as to which direction I started out in. Instead I stepped forward again into the next mirror. This was a really bad one, altering the way I felt about myself. *I'm wrong! I'm always wrong! I can't make a good decision!* I felt the mirror turning me uncertain and indecisive, making me feel that no matter what I did next, I was doomed, doomed, doomed.

Maggie felt it too. I heard her moaning and trying to loosen her grip on my hand, not trusting me, not trusting herself. If I gave in to those feelings, we truly would be doomed, so I fought my own mind and made my feet move, stepping forward again through the next mirror, and the next, and the next, always moving forward. My stride became a limping lope; my eyesight turned cloudy and full of double images as my eyes changed sizes.

Through it all, Maggie held my hand. At the times when I came to mirrors that slowed me down because of what they made me feel, that was when she took the lead, pulling me on, even when I didn't have the strength to move forward.

There came a point when my body had become so unnaturally bent and convoluted that moving forward was next to impossible. One foot dragged, the other moved sideways. My whole body ached and strained against itself as if, at any moment, my joints would give way and I would collapse into a blubbery mess on the bone-ridden ground. My own frame looked as bad as these bones did, and I wondered whether they were actually the bones of other unfortunate riders or whether they were just put here to force everyone trapped in the maze to give up hope. We must have passed through twenty mirrors. I began to worry that maybe my theory was wrong.

I stumbled, and Maggie helped me up. I felt my face and turned to her. She didn't look much worse than she had when I first found her, but then, she couldn't look much worse than she already had.

"Now we're the same," I told her. My voice was so distorted, I could barely make out my own words.

She touched my face, which was numb and rubbery. "We always were," she said.

Do you know what it's like to be turned inside out in every way you can be and have the worst parts of yourself exposed to anyone who happens to be looking? Maybe you do—after all, it happens to us a little bit all the time. I guess lots of people would look at you and run, like Russ. But to have someone who won't run—someone who won't use your shame against you—that takes someone special. Having that person with you in the worst part of the maze makes all the difference.

I honestly don't know if I could have made it any farther on my own, but Maggie was there, and it was all right. We were the same.

I took her hand again and kept going. If moving through the mirrors was a mistake, I didn't care. I was going all the way, until there was nothing left of me. We pushed through five more mirrors. Ten. Twenty. Then finally the reflections started to get just a little bit better. The feelings I had inside began to lighten just the slightest bit.

A few mirrors more, and my eyes went back to normal, the twist in my spine was almost gone, and my arms were just about the same length. I was almost myself, and when I looked to Maggie, she was almost herself again too.

Finally we stood at the last mirror. I knew it was the last mirror because the reflection it gave back was perfect. Well, maybe not perfect, but me, in all my imperfections. As I stood there I felt the urge to look anywhere but straight ahead, as if the mirrors on either side of me were daring me to take a final glance. I resisted. I forced myself to take that giant step through the last mirror, to find myself facing a pea green sky and an endless salt flat.

"We made it!" I shouted. "We're out!"

. . . But somewhere along the way, as we were passing through those last few mirrors, I'd let go of Maggie's hand. When I looked beside me, Maggie wasn't there. I turned around and saw her standing just on the other side of the final mirror. It was one-way. She couldn't see me, but I could see her.

"Maggie, come on! Step through!" She couldn't hear me, either, so I reached out—and bumped against glass. From my side, the mirror was solid.

"Blake?" she called. "Blake . . . where are you?"

"*Maggie!*" I screamed, and I pounded on the glass, but she couldn't see, she couldn't hear!

"Blake?"

And then she turned.

I don't know what she saw in the mirror beside her, but whatever it was, it must have been horrible. It must have been the worst mirror of all, because it undid her. She put her hand over her mouth and let loose a wail so full of despair, it could blacken the sun.

"Turn around!" I yelled at her. "Look forward. Just one more step—just one more!"

But she couldn't hear me. I pounded on the glass again and again, but nothing helped. She was locked on whatever she was seeing.

She stumbled back and fell through another mirror. I watched, powerless, as she looked around, trying to remember from which way she had come. She was sobbing now. Sorrow, fear, all her worst emotions were amplified, stretching her face again as she stumbled in one direction and then another and another.

"Maggie!"

I kept my eyes locked on her, pounding on the glass as she ran in a panic in every direction, passing through mirror after mirror, becoming more and more distorted and disoriented, her screams changing until they weren't even human. Then she was gone, so lost in the maze that I couldn't see her anymore.

"Nooo!" I beat the glass again with all my might. I wanted the glass to shatter—I wanted the whole cathedral to explode—but the glass held. I slid to the ground, and for the first time since arriving in this terrible place, I cried. I bawled like a baby. It was all my fault! I'd let her go. I'd stepped out before she had, and now she was lost and alone. I'd left her. Despite all my promises, I'd left her. Suddenly I felt the way I did all those years ago, when I had pounded against the emergency exit door at the back of the bus, unable to open it.

To be completely helpless in the face of life—powerless to do a single thing—that's what I'd always feared more than anything. It was like I'd been keeping all the edges of my life neat and clean, pretending the neatness was all that mattered, pretending life could somehow be controlled.

For a moment I felt like giving up. I closed my eyes. No. I would not give in. If it was my fate to keep smashing my fist against emergency exit doors, then that's what I would do. Even if I saved no one. Even if I died doing it, this place would not beat me.

I opened my eyes. There before me on the barren salt plain was a turnstile in front of a freestanding stone arch. My failure to bring Maggie out of the maze weighed on me like an anchor, but I buried my feelings of loss, of inadequacy, and of failure. Those mirrors were behind me now. My path was forward. It had to be. Four rides down. I was more than halfway to seven. I put one foot in front of the other, forcing myself to move on, refusing to look back.

As I walked away from the distortions of the mirrored cathedral, the symbol on the back of my hand glowed blinding white, and for the first time I felt excitement instead of just dread. I was not going to be a victim; I was a challenger, just as Cassandra had said. I was going to be the best challenger this place had ever known.

I ran my hand over the scanner and pushed through the turnstile. I was no longer on the salt flat but was winding through an empty line, toward the ride ahead. I heard the ride before I saw it—an awful metallic *click-click-click* of a chain. I knew that sound. Oh, did I know that sound.

The next ride was a roller coaster. And it was called the Kamikaze.

9

Zero Tolerance

The coaster looked like a replica of the Kamikaze roller coaster I rode last night, back in the amusement park where people didn't get killed—or, at least, didn't get killed on purpose. There were two major differences to this coaster, however. First, there was only one seat in each row, not two. Nobody rode with a partner. On *this* Kamikaze everyone rode alone. Second, the steep climb didn't stop where it was supposed to; it just kept going up into a bright blue sky speckled with clouds. I looked at my watch again: 4:15. Still long before dawn in the real world.

As with all the other rides, there were a dozen or so kids weaving through the maze of the line. They didn't see each other, didn't see anything but the ride. It filled their minds and spirits. They were already owned by this place and didn't know it.

By the time I reached the front, the train was full. The ride operator was standing in front of a huge lever that grew from the ground. He had a sick leer on his face, like he'd just done something he wouldn't tell his momma about. He also had only one arm—his left one—which was strong and muscular, I assume from working this lever since the beginning of time.

"Room up front," he said to me, and let out a noise that was something between a giggle and sucking up snot.

I took another look at the train. Like I said, it was completely full.

"Sorry, Lefty. Guess I'll have to ride the next one."

The guy looked at the kid sitting in the first car and grabbed him by the front of his shirt. With a single tug, he launched the kid skyward. I never actually saw that kid come down.

"Room up front," Lefty said again, and smiled that I-got-bodies-in-my-freezer kind of smile.

"Yeah. Funny I didn't notice it before," I said, and took my place. *Okay, I'm ready for this,* I told myself, as if thinking it would make it so. Just a few minutes ago I was full of piss and vinegar, as my mom would say. But now I was just about ready to let loose some of the first ingredient in my jeans. Did it *have* to be a roller coaster?

I pulled down the safety bar, but it kept popping right back up.

"Hey, wait a second!"

Too late. Lefty grabbed the huge lever, hauled on it, and away we rolled, cranking up the insanely steep climb toward a windswept sky.

It took at least ten minutes to reach the top. My hands were freezing as I tugged on that stupid lap bar, which still refused to stay down. The peak rose above the clouds, and beneath it a massive lattice of wood dropped out of sight to the ground, which looked like it was a mile or two below us. In the world I came from, no one could build a structure like that, but here in Cassandra's worlds there were all sorts of mystical feats of engineering.

My heart sped up, aching in my chest. What would the ride become once it began its first drop? *Maybe it's just a roller coaster,* I tried to tell myself. *A really BIG roller coaster.*

As we reached the peak I turned to see the kids behind me putting their hands up in the air. That's when I noticed the clouds below weren't just random shapes. There were faces in them.

The drop came into view as we crested the peak. And then the train began its fall.

My teeth rattled in my skull, and my brain felt like it would come loose in my head. We were not just being pulled by gravity, we were accelerating faster than gravity could possibly pull us. I felt the skin on my face stretched by g-forces as we dove into the clouds. And then things began to change. The ride began to take on its true form.

The little space for my legs stretched as it had in the bumper cars, but the dashboard in front of me didn't expand into the dashboard of a car. It became an instrument panel with dozens of knobs, buttons, and screens. A glass canopy grew over me, sealing me in, and the clatter of the track changed pitch, becoming the whine of an engine.

A stick with two handles grew from the floorboard, and when I looked to the side, I could see wings stretching out from under me: wings with a bright red spot painted on each one.

This was a plane, and I was flying it.

I tried to crane my head around to see the kids behind me, and I saw enough to know that the train had broken apart into twelve separate cockpits. I was alone in my own propeller aircraft—the first in a line of a dozen planes plunging down through the clouds.

I flashed on an image of my American Airlines ticket to New York tucked so peacefully away in my desk drawer back home. All of a sudden an airline meal and an in-flight movie didn't sound so bad.

Okay . . . okay, I told myself, trying to rein in my panic. *So I'm flying a plane. I can do this. So what if I've never flown a plane before? So what if hundreds of people die every year in air disasters? I can figure this out, right? I can read all the markings on the instruments and figure out what they all do, right?*

Well, maybe not. Because everything was labeled in Japanese.

That's when it occurred to me exactly what kind of plane had big red spots painted on the wings. And why the ride was called the Kamikaze.

I've got a Japanese Zero in my room—or at least a model of one, perfectly glued and painted. Just like the real thing, with one big exception: The Zero in my bedroom wasn't about to kill me.

My Zero shuddered violently as I dove down into the

cloud bank, the other planes trailing behind me. A few seconds later we were through the clouds. The ground came into focus. . . . Only it wasn't ground at all, it was ocean. More specifically, the Pacific Ocean, and I was headed toward a little cigar-shaped gray thing in the water.

It only took a moment for my brain to get up to speed and adjust for scale. That little gray thing wasn't so little after all. It was far away but getting closer. It was, in fact, a battleship. As I recalled from my old Battleship game, it took four direct hits to sink a battleship. As I recalled from my World War II history, countless American ships were brutally disabled by pilots of the "Divine Wind" making suicide runs, crashing their planes into battleships, cruisers, destroyers, and even aircraft carriers.

I knew enough from Quinn's flight-simulator games to know that you pull back on the stick to make the plane go up, and so I grabbed both grips and pulled. The stick shuddered and resisted, as uncooperative as that stupid lap bar had been. The other planes buzzed behind me, and all at once I realized I was not just one of a dozen planes, I was the squadron leader. They were all following me to their doom.

Once more this place had tapped into my secret fears. Fear of flying, fear of falling, but even worse than that, the fear of taking everyone down with me.

The battleship swelled before me as I dove toward it. Now I could see sailors scrambling on the deck, manning their big guns, and firing in my direction.

They say when you're about to die, your life flashes before your eyes, but that's not quite right. It isn't the flickering of life's events that strikes you; instead, it's the sudden realization of what your life has *meant*. Your whole life is captured in a single image that tells you who you've been. The image that came to me now were those stupid models hanging in my bedroom. The Zero, chased by a P-40, frozen in a pretend dogfight dive.

That was my life.

I hadn't lived a real life—I'd had just a *model* of a life. Everything I did, everything I *thought*, was suspended safely by strings, too high up for anyone to damage. Zero contact, zero risk. Now those strings had been cut and I was going to die, never having had a chance to live without them.

A blast exploded to my right as the battleship's guns tried to take me out. The shock wave rattled my plane. I could see the bridge of the battleship now. Crewmen inside were running for cover.

There was little time left if I was going to survive this ride. I had to put away thoughts of life and death and focus on this moment. I had to live through this moment so there could be a next one. I had the strength to do that much.

I will not crash, I told myself. *I will not go down in a burst of flames. I won't go down at all!* I pulled back on the steering column with the strength of that conviction, and finally it began to move. Before me the battleship fell away as my plane, and all the planes behind me, pulled out of the kamikaze dive into a parabolic arc. All the planes, that is, except for the last one. The last plane just kept going and hit the battleship, detonating in a fireball. I felt sick. *Don't be Quinn*, I prayed. It would be just like him to crash on purpose, just like he did on his flight simulator back home.

Then, above me, as I climbed away from the battleship, I saw a new cloud billowing up. A face appeared, eyes locked in shock and disbelief. A face that wasn't Quinn's.

No strings, I told myself. I was flying with no strings, and I was no longer afraid. Like it or not, I was in charge, and there was no room for fear. I tried to get control of the plane as it lurched and spun, and I imagined the planes behind me following my motions, like they were still on a roller-coaster track, but I was the one determining the path.

Suddenly the control stick flew out of my grip and forced itself forward. The ride had taken control again, and we had started another dive. This time we were headed toward a destroyer. It began shooting at us. One of its shells took out a plane behind me. I watched it spiral a flaming path to the sea.

I fought the controls, my will straining against the will of the ride. Once again, I was able to pull up, gaining altitude at the last second, climbing away from the destroyer. Once again, the last plane didn't pull up in time and detonated on the deck. In an instant we were back in the clouds, but by now I'd gotten a feel for the controls. It was kind of like driving a car with really bad steering. Well, okay, it was more like *skydiving* in a car with really bad steering, but at least I could make the thing move the way I wanted it to.

I heard another explosion and looked out of the window to see one of the planes in my care fall in flames. That blast hadn't come from below.

Another plane pulled up beside me, matching my speed, its wingtip almost touching mine. It was the American P-40 from my bedroom, with the face of a shark painted on its air intake. Its pilot waved to me.

"A great day for flying," said Cassandra's voice over my radio. I should have known.

"Nothing like the friendly skies," I radioed back, then I jinked to the right, into a corkscrew, with all the planes behind me still following my lead. Cassandra fired at me. I felt more than heard her rounds tear into the tail of my Zero, but I didn't lose control. The ride hadn't taken me down, so she was going to do it herself.

A tight bank, and I was able to position myself right behind her. It didn't take a Columbia scholarship to figure out how to fire my machine guns. I let them rip, tearing into her wing. The damage wasn't enough to take her down, but it was enough to let her know I wasn't going out without a fight.

"You're shooting at an American plane," her voice crackled over the radio. "How unpatriotic."

"Sorry, I don't speak English," I told her. "I'm a Japanese pilot."

She pulled her plane out of sight, and I wasn't sure where she was until I heard her machine gun fire. The plane right behind me fell away, plunging to the sea, trailing a plume of smoke. I dove, banked, and spun to get away, leading the remaining planes out of the path of Cassandra's guns. She fired again but missed.

"You're a fantastic squadron leader, Blake. This ride has never been so exciting!" She stormed me from above, leaning on her guns, tearing up my right wing. "You're a true warrior," she said. "There's no greater challenge than a survivor."

No one had ever called me a warrior before. At any other time I might have felt full of myself, but this wasn't any other time.

I tried to maneuver, but my plane was too badly damaged. She fired again, shredding my left wing. My gauges dropped suddenly. My engine began to miss, then caught fire, and my plane began a doomed spiral toward the sea.

I didn't know whether or not the other planes still followed my lead or if I had fallen out of formation when I took the damage. All I could see was black smoke billowing from my engine, but through that smoke, I caught glimpses of an aircraft carrier directly below.

"It's a noble death," Cassandra said. "An end worthy of a pilot of the Divine Wind."

And then Cassandra's own words came back to me. *There's a way out of every ride.*

Without intending to, she had provided the means of my salvation. My plane was crashing, no doubt about that now. But there was a way out of every ride. Even this one.

The cockpit smelled of gasoline and smoke, and a

bitter taste filled my mouth, like I'd been chewing on rubber. The engine had stopped completely. I looked frantically around the cockpit for a way out of the ride, pounding on the canopy, searching in front of me, below me, behind me. I was disoriented and dizzy from the spiraling of the Zero, but I wasn't giving up.

"Good-bye, Blake," and she sighed, as if sorry to see the hunt end. "It was worth the risk to bring you here."

There's a way out of every ride . . . a way out of every ride, I chanted to myself over and over. A hundred knobs covered the dashboard, but I had no idea what they did because they were all marked with Japanese symbols.

Except one.

Seconds from impact, I spotted it. The ride symbol was right there on a little button hidden in a corner of the instrument panel. Ha! I didn't wait to think about it. I hit the button.

Boom! The canopy tore away, my seat ejected into the sky, and the plane crashed into the tower of the aircraft carrier. Shrapnel from the explosion shot past me. The heat singed my eyebrows, but I was out! I was out and rocketing skyward. No strings, no ceiling to hang them from. I'd been cut loose, and I was still alive. I *was* a survivor, and nothing had ever felt so good.

Your own words saved me, Cassandra. Who's the winner now?

A hole opened up in the sky like the iris of a camera, and I shot through, out of the world of the Kamikaze.

10
Depraved Heart

Last year I did a term paper on cancer. Cancer is such a sneaky disease because it starts inside, hiding in the body, turning the body's own cells into the enemy. *Insidious*—that's the word for it—sneaky and subtle and evil all at the same time. It just keeps growing and growing, because the body doesn't know how to wage war against itself. That's the way the park worked. It dug into your thoughts and pulled these worlds right out of them. Your own mind became the enemy, and how can you fight your own mind? The only difference is that cancer doesn't have a soul. I don't know which was harder to face: the soullessness of a tumor, or Cassandra, the spirit of a malignant park.

She'd done her best to take me out on the Kamikaze, and had almost succeeded, but I was still standing. Well, actually I was floating, with a parachute above me and the lights of the amusement park below me. I thought that after ejecting from the Kamikaze, I'd have to swim the South Pacific to find the next ride. Instead, I'd been sent back to where I'd started: the crossroads of all the rides—the place where my world met Cassandra's. I wondered why.

I landed in the midway, hitting the ground hard and feeling the pain of the impact in my joints. The chute settled down around me, and I had to fight my way out of it, pulling back on the silk. As I tried to pull the shroud of the parachute away, I saw a second figure moving toward me in the billowing fabric, like a ghost. Had I come down on some other rider? Was it Cassandra?

I pulled the parachute away. It was Russ. I didn't know who was more relieved, him or me.

"You're alive!" he said. "This place hasn't chewed you up!"

"Well, I kinda keep kicking it in the teeth whenever it tries."

The relief in seeing him faded quickly when I thought about Maggie and how he'd run from her in the maze.

"So where's Maggie?" I asked, just to see if he'd squirm.

"Lost her," he said.

Should I confront him about it right here? I decided against it. I looked at the amusement park around us. There were still some riders milling around, latecomers seeking out their first ride, but the crowds had been absorbed by the attractions.

"Until now the rides have all connected to one another," I said. "So how come we're here and not in another ride?"

"Like I know?"

There was something strange about Russ. A kind of fear in the way he looked at me. A twitch in his cheek. The rides had stressed me almost to my breaking point, and when I last saw Russ, he was already pushing his. Funny, but I always thought Russ could take care of himself.

I checked my watch: 4:40. Only two rides to go, and time was running out. Maybe he'd abandoned Maggie, but I didn't have it in me to abandon him. "We'll stick together," I told him, "and make sure we don't separate again."

"Okay, fine."

"The rides are tough, but we can be tougher."

"Okay, fine."

"Remember that there's a way off of every ride."

"No problem."

He was so agreeable, it was sad. This place had whipped him, wiped him, and hung him out to dry. I led the way, trying to second-guess what the rides around us might be. "Do you think we should try—"

A sharp explosion of pain on the side of my head. I was on the ground before I knew what hit me, clapping my hand to my aching ear. It was swelling, but my ear had cushioned the blow, protecting my skull. I looked up to see Russ holding a steel pole. It looked like one of the levers that operated the rides.

"I'm sorry, Blake, but I gotta do what I gotta do."

There were tears in his eyes, but they didn't stop him from swinging that pole again. I dodged, and it caught my upper arm; the bone didn't break, but I could feel the pain of the blow from my shoulder to my fingertips. I scrambled away, but Russ still stalked me.

"She's gonna let me go." Russ's face was red from anguish. "You understand, right? I gotta do this, so Cassandra'll let me out of here. She promised." Russ swung again, but this time he missed. It gave me the time I needed to get to my feet and bolt.

My head was still reeling from that first blow. I couldn't think straight, and I didn't know which way to run, so after rounding a corner I ducked into one of those automated photo booths—the kind you squeeze into with your friends, when they're not trying to kill you. I pulled the curtain and peeked out, hoping I could throw Russ off the track long enough for me to recover physically, and mentally. Through the curtain, I saw him wandering the midway.

"Blake! Don't make this harder than it has to be!"

I took a few deep breaths as I came to grips with the situation. At home Russ lacked the conviction to do much of anything but hang out and wisecrack. But when it came to killing his best friend to save his own hide, he suddenly found deep motivation.

"You know I'll find you, Blake. You won't get away. But I'm sorry. I'm really, really sorry about this."

Was it really Russ? I tried to tell myself that it was a false image of him, like Carl and the whale with my mother's eyes. But who was I kidding? This was no false image. This was Russ through and through. The place had gotten to him. *She* had gotten to him. The next time he passed the booth, I leaped out suddenly, knocking him down. The pole clattered to the ground, and I grabbed it. Now it was me standing over him with the pole in my hand.

"Don't . . . move."

He froze and stared at me, waiting to see what I'd do. I wasn't even sure myself. I was so furious. I was tempted to smash him, just as he'd smashed me, but then he put his head in his hands and started crying like a baby. Still I hung on to that pole, not knowing how to feel.

I'd once read about a type of crime called "depraved heart murder." Few people ever get charged with it, but in the story there was this guy who was on a sinking boat. He couldn't swim, so he panicked and ripped a life vest away from a seven-year-old girl. The little girl drowned.

Depraved heart. He got twenty to life.

What do you feel for a coward like that? What should I feel for someone who would kill his best friend to save his own life?

"I'm sorry, man . . . I'm sorry," Russ said through his tears.

I found I had no response to that.

"Cassandra promised she'd let me out. All I had to do . . . all I had to do . . ."

"Was kill me?"

His face went an ugly shade of red.

"You didn't ride the Ferris wheel!" he screamed. "You don't know what it does to you! I can't take another ride! If you rode the Ferris wheel, you'd know!"

But I couldn't imagine any ride that would make me

slam a pole through my best friend's skull. They say you never know who's the real hero and who's the real coward until you're looking death in the face. I've always been afraid of plenty of things, but fear isn't what makes you a coward. It's how depraved your heart becomes when fear gets pumped through it. I would never climb over the backs of my friends to save myself.

Russ looked around nervously, as if Cassandra might swoop down out of the sky and swallow him whole. "I'm not letting this place get me like it got Maggie." He started to take off.

"Russ, wait!" I don't know why I tried to stop him when I really just wanted him out of my sight. I guess I'm a pathological fixer. I can't let anyone or anything just be; I've got to try to make it better. "Where do you think you're going to run?"

"This place has to have a way out! We're not stuck in a ride now, so we've got to be closer to getting out!"

"What do you think, you'll just find the back door and skip through?"

"I won't get on another ride!" He pushed me away, and then he looked down one of the many connecting aisles of the park. "Do—do you see that!"

It was a revolving door with a big happy face above it, and stamped on the happy face's forehead were the words:

EXIT
COME AGAIN SOON!
TELL YOUR FRIENDS!

Russ ran toward it without a second thought. But there was something wrong. It was too easy. . . .

"Russ, wait!" I tried to catch him, but I hurt so much from the beating he'd given me, I couldn't move fast enough.

Russ never saw it coming. He had no idea.

The dusty ground of the park fell away beneath him as a trapdoor opened with a loud bang. He screamed and dropped down into a hole. I got there a moment too late, but not too late to get a look. The hole had opened into a vast pit full of shiny chrome gears, cogs and pistons, thrown together at weird, impossible angles, all cranking in overdrive.

The Works.

I felt that if I looked too long, I'd fall in too.

Rising heat singed my nostrils, and the smell of burning grease made my throat close up. I couldn't see Russ anymore, couldn't even hear his screams over the grinding of the massive machine. It was as if he'd been ground up in it, his essence becoming oil for the gears.

The trapdoor sprang closed. When I looked up, I saw two park workers grab the "exit door" and roll it away, revealing a brick wall behind it. It was just a facade.

"Gets 'em every time," Cassandra said.

I whirled on her. "You couldn't take me on yourself?" I screamed, my teeth bared like a wild animal. "You had to bring Russ into it?"

"I needed a champion to defeat the dragon. I chose him."

"And I'm the dragon?"

"So it seems."

"*You* were the one who destroyed him. Not me." I took a good look at her. She stood so casually in the middle of the midway, dressed in simple jeans and a blouse—the way I'd first seen her when she gave me the stuffed bear and my personal invitation. But was I imagining it, or was something different about her now? She looked . . . wary. Could it be apprehension? Uncertainty? It wasn't just her, but the park as well. I could suddenly hear it in the calliope music all around us, which sounded just a little flat and off-key, like it was slowly winding down. The park seemed to be losing some of its integrity and coherence.

But why? It couldn't have been because of anything I'd done. All I'd done was make it through five rides.

Five rides. With only two left to go. Then something occurred to me. . . .

"No one's ever made it this far, have they?"

Cassandra didn't answer, but she didn't have to. I knew. I was the first one to get this far! What was it she had said before my Zero crashed? *It was worth the risk to bring you here.* The risk of what?

"What happens if I make it through all seven rides?" I asked, moving toward her. "Is this place like a video game that shuts down when somebody beats it? Is that what happens?"

She couldn't look me in the eye. "I don't know what happens."

I was face-to-face with her now. "What you're feeling now, *that's* fear," I told her. "Is it all you imagined it would be?"

127

She pulled back, speechless. I was more than a challenge to her now. I was a threat—perhaps the only one she had ever faced, and I still couldn't understand why.

Her eyes clouded with hatred. "You really should be dead, Blake."

"Maybe your rides are just too easy."

"I'm not talking about the rides. I think you know that."

And there was a part of me that did know.

I should be dead. I should have been dead a long, long time ago.

I thought back to the bumper cars, and finally something clicked. It was no coincidence that Cassandra had seemed so familiar to me when I first saw her, and that vision I had gotten of an orange sports car when she had sped past me in old Chicago wasn't a hallucination. It was a memory.

"You were there!"

Cassandra smiled.

"You—You drove a sports car! You pulled in front of our bus, cutting it off, and that's why the driver lost control. You made the bus crash!" My heart began to outrace my brain. I didn't know which would explode first. *"You're the one who set the whole thing in motion!"*

I didn't know how it could be, and yet I knew that it was true.

Cassandra's fear was all but gone now. "What I want to know is how you managed to survive."

I couldn't look at her, so I looked down at the ride symbol on the back of my hand. It had all started ten years ago. Cassandra hadn't singled me out tonight, I'd been on her list since the day of the bus accident.

Because I had survived when I wasn't supposed to.

I knew what I had to do.

"Get out of my way," I told her. "I've got two more rides."

As I pushed past her my arm brushed hers, and I got another impression of her true form—that strange sensation of intense heat encased in intense cold, the living embodiment of two opposing extremes—and it finally occurred to me why I, of all people, was able to battle her!

Perhaps I am the balance! Maybe I was the one human being smack in the middle between her two extremes. And if there was anything that Cassandra could not abide, it was balance.

11

The Wheel of Ra

There was no easy choice as to which ride to take next. The ones that seemed to lure me were the ones most likely to trap me. On the other hand, the rides that gave me the worst feeling must have made me feel that way for a reason. I finally settled on the Wheel of Ra as my next ride, mainly because I had no feeling about it either way. It was what you would call a "vomit ride." You know the kind—you get inside what's basically a big drum that spins you around and around, gluing you up against the wall with centrifugal force and making you so nauseous that you end up puking things you probably ate in previous lives.

The wheel itself had an Egyptian theme: There were pictures of guys with their shoulders turned sideways and hieroglyphics adorned in gold.

As I approached the turnstile my feet felt heavy. It was hard to move forward, as if a wind were pushing against me, but the air was dead still. I figured it was just the park trying to slow me down and prevent me from finishing my sixth ride. My arm on the turnstile felt like lead; I could barely lift it. I fought gravity, got my hand high enough to slide it across the scanner, and forced my way through the resisting stile.

Something's wrong, I told myself, and then told myself to shut up. Of course something was wrong. *Everything* was wrong in this place.

"Have you ever been on this ride before?" asked a clueless kid in front of me as we stepped up to the wheel. The kid looked a little nervous. His eyes were so big, he looked like something from one of those Japanese cartoons.

"On it *before*? This must be your first ride."

The kid shrugged. "Well, the lines were too long everywhere else. I couldn't pick which one to go on first, so I've just been walking around most of the night."

I wanted to offer the kid some advice, but I couldn't think of anything to tell him.

"I hope it's not too fast," he said as he took his place in the wheel beside me. I looked across the circle at the other riders. They were all excited and mesmerized in anticipation of their next thrill.

It was only as the wheel began to grind into motion that it occurred to me why this ride felt so terribly wrong.

This was not my ride.

The symbol hadn't been glowing when I swiped it over the scanner. The turnstile didn't want to admit me because this wasn't a ride meant for me. Was that to my advantage, or would it only make the ride harder? I'd find out soon enough, because the ride had begun, and I was committed to seeing it through. The lights around me now spun and strobed, making the eyes on the Egyptian pictographs appear to move. I was pressed against the wall, feeling dizzier by the second.

This is not my ride!

Faster and faster. I saw glimpses of the outside world though the slits in the drum, like one of those old-fashioned spinning movie drums. A zoetrope, it's called. Through those slits, I saw the world change. The predawn black sky of the amusement park turned a rich indigo blue.

The ride never felt like it actually slowed, but the world stopped spinning around it. We were no longer pressed against the padded walls of the wheel. In fact, there was no padding behind us at all. We were standing against the stone pillars of a circular temple, and the pictographs that had been decorating the walls had become Egyptian warriors, each with more muscles than those Russian guys that lift eighteen-wheelers on the Extreme Sports Channel. They began to round us up with whips and brute force.

"Don't let them catch you!" I shouted.

"Well, duh!" said a girl dressed in filthy rags. Actually we were all dressed in filthy rags. Our costumes for the ride.

The other riders raced around the temple in confusion, trying to get away, but the guards must have been through this a thousand times. They caught each rider easily, rounding them all up, shackling them at the ankles, and forcing them to the ground.

I saw an unguarded opening between two pillars. It was my chance to get away, but as I began to run, I saw the clueless kid—the one with the buggy cartoon eyes—with a whip wrapped around his neck, held by a monster of a guard with the neck of a linebacker, who looked mighty fierce, even in a skirt.

The kid's eyes bulged even more than they had before.

I cursed my stupid conscience, then I raced over to the kid, grabbed the whip, and unwrapped it from his neck. The guard looked at me like I was a quarterback he was about to sack. He was too big to fight, but guys that big can also be clumsy. Still holding the end of his whip, I ran straight toward him, then, at the last second, I slid beneath his legs, coming out the other side. He didn't let go of the whip, which is what I was counting on. My momentum pulled the whip and his arm between his own legs, leaving him off balance. I rammed into him, toppling him, then I wrapped his own whip around his muscle-bound neck and pulled tight until *his* eyes were the ones bulging. Touchdown!

And then I heard another kid behind me.

"Kill the creep," he said.

"Yeah," said another.

I could have done it. The guard was gasping for breath, and, as strong as he was, he couldn't pry me loose. But the malice in those kids' voices got to me. Rather than finishing him off, I let him go.

By now I'd attracted the attention of the other guards, but the rest of the kids were getting some nerve of their own and fought back. Some of them had already been captured, but more managed to get away, running from the hilltop temple in all directions.

I ran until I knew I'd outrun my pursuers. Then I stopped to take in my surroundings. It had to be the most spectacular of Cassandra's worlds. It was Egypt, but not the real Egypt. It was an exaggerated, absurd vision of everything you might imagine Egypt to have been in its glory but many times larger than life. To the north the Pyramids of Giza towered into the sky. The Great Pyramid's solid gold tip shone like an illuminatus—you know, that pyramid eye on the back of a dollar bill. It shone against a twilight sky painted in hues of deep indigo blue. The entire sky looked like a bruise across heaven.

In the valley before me, along the bank of the Nile, stood a great city of stone and gold. Hundreds of workers hauled massive stones and obelisks. They were also dressed in tattered rags, but the shirts on their backs were bloodied and torn by the whips of their brutal taskmasters. Cassandra had said that these worlds were built on the souls of those trapped here. Watching this human machine of construction, I believed it.

I hid behind stones and scaffolds, darting in and out of shadows, trying to keep out of the taskmasters' lines of sight. This was not my ride. There was no place for me here, no secret terror to tackle. All I had to do was pass through the city undetected and find the seventh ride.

At the edge of the city a team of workers pulled on

ropes, dragging a statue that lay on its back. It was the statue of a pharaoh, his stone image decorated with diamonds and silver. Even lying on its back, the statue was two stories high, and the workers dragging it couldn't move it more than a few inches at a time. When the coast was clear, I darted into the gilded city, where more workers labored joylessly, setting tiny jewels into the lines of pictographs. It was a world of opulence, that was clear. But for whose benefit?

"Idols here!" a voice shouted, and I turned to see, of all things, a street vendor. He held a tray before him like a peanut vendor at a baseball game. "Get your idols here! Ra . . . Horus . . . graven image of Tutankhamen, king a' da Nile—better likeness here than on the Great Sphinx."

"The face on the Great Sphinx isn't King Tut's," I told him, sounding way too much like a know-it-all.

"It is here," he said. He glanced at my filthy clothing. "Escaped from the mud pits, huh?" he said. "Good for you. Better change out of those clothes, or you'll be caught for sure. I wouldn't want to be in your sandals then."

"Can you tell me where the next ride is?"

He laughed at me. "I just sell idols, kid."

"But you didn't always sell idols. You were once a kid like me, weren't you? How many years have you been here, playacting for Cassandra?"

He looked at me sternly, like we were on stage and I'd forgotten my part. "Do you want an idol or not?"

"If you help me, I'll be the first one to make it through," I told him. "I'm on my sixth ride."

"Yeah, right, and I'm Cleopatra." Then he turned and continued on, shouting, "Idols here!"

I was about to let him go, but my mind hooked on something I had seen on his tray. *No—it can't be what it looked like,* I told myself. *It's just coincidence, right? Just my mind playing tricks on me. It has to be!* I hurried after him, and he sighed, figuring I was going to keep on pressing him for information.

"I want to see your idols."

"Forget it. You can't afford anything I have, anyway."

"So what? I still want to see them."

Wanting more than ever to be rid of me, he held up a jade cobra. "Tell you what. You can have this one for free. It's Wadjet, the protector of kings. Guaranteed to bring you luck—although not always good."

I wasn't interested in the cobra. Instead, I picked up a gold statue of a pharaoh.

"That's my best-seller," said the vendor. "King Tut. He brings good fortune to crops and livestock. No plagues or your money back."

My hand shook as I held the little statue. The graven image was well carved. Its likeness was perfect.

I turned around, looking back toward the team of slaves in the distance; they were still pulling the giant statue on its back. Only the statue's profile was visible, but the likeness was unmistakable. As I looked around I found the image of the king everywhere—in the jeweled artwork of the buildings and on the sides of the towering obelisks.

The vendor grabbed the little statue back. "Out of

your price range, kid. No freebies on Tut."

Something he'd said came back to me. I turned to the north, where, between the jagged points of pyramids, I found the Great Sphinx. Its body was the crouching form of a lion, but its face was that of a pharaoh . . . a pharaoh whose stony face was adorned with silver earrings and nose rings and a ring jammed diagonally through his eyebrow. Just like the actual person.

Just like Quinn.

"The boy king," said the vendor. "Gotta love 'im. His reign is always short, but believe me, it's intense."

"That's my brother!"

The vendor was only slightly moved. "Lucky him."

My head was spinning, and I stumbled back against a wall to steady myself. My brother was King Tut. It gave whole new meaning to the term *vomit ride.*

"This slave insists on having an audience with you."

A brawny guard hurled me into a great room fifty yards long. A carpet of rose petals filled the chamber with a sweet rich aroma as I treaded toward a raised platform. Quinn was there, all right. He reclined on a silk settee while musicians played strange stringed instruments alongside him and richly dressed courtiers talked to one another, filling their plates with food piled high on a long table. Quinn didn't come to the table; instead, beautiful women encircled him, feeding him from silver platters. He was dressed like a pharaoh, from the top of his gold and turquoise headdress to the soles of his sandals. I, on the other hand, still wore rags that smelled so badly of mildew and sweat that not even the rising aroma of roses could mask the stench.

Quinn saw me and sat up. "Hey, bro! Look who got the best seat on the ride!"

Our last encounter had been a hard awakening for me, having to face Quinn's desperation and emptiness. I wasn't sure this was any better. Quinn the god: emperor of all he surveyed.

A guard grabbed me by the neck, forcing me to my knees. The rose petals did little to cushion my kneecaps from the stone ground below.

"Humble yourself before Pharaoh."

"No, it's okay," said Quinn. "Allow the slave to approach."

Reluctantly the guard removed his hand from my neck and let me rise. I stepped up to the raised dais, where Quinn luxuriated like a pig in a very expensive poke. He grinned and held up the pharaoh's crook—the hooked scepter of the kings. "Hey, check out the back scratcher! You won't find *that* at The Sharper Image!"

He was so full of this fantasy—so drunk on it—that I didn't know if there was any way to reach him. It was like he was dangling from the hanging roller-coaster rails again, never seeing the train coming around the bend until it was too late. *I can't save you, Quinn. I can't save you from yourself.* That's what I wanted to say, but no words came out.

He was all smiles. "Speechless, huh? I'm not surprised."

"Time's running out," I finally said. "It's almost dawn."

He looked to a huge window framing the timeless and unchanging indigo sky. "It doesn't look like dawn to me."

"No—I mean in the real world. The place that matters."

Quinn looked around furtively, then leaned in close, so that no one else could hear. "Don't ruin this for me!" he said. And I saw, behind all the glitz and dazzle Quinn had surrounded himself with, that hollow desperation that was always there. "You have your life," he whispered, "your grades, your scholarship. Let me have *this*."

How could I argue against that craving in him, that bottomless need for something more? "Quinn . . . whatever you think is happening here, you're wrong. No matter how empty you feel inside, this place won't fill you. It's like . . . cotton candy, and in the end it'll destroy you."

Quinn looked around at his court, where dozens of subjects filled the great hall, ready to bow to his every whim. "If I have to spend my life trapped on a ride, then I'm fine with this one." He leaned back on his settee and motioned to one of the slave girls, who fed him more candied dates. "The mighty Tutankhamen moves for no man," he said, loud enough for his subjects to hear.

"The mighty Tutankhamen was killed by his adviser!"

"That's never been proven," said a familiar voice. I turned to see Cassandra step out from behind a pillar.

"Meet my adviser," said Quinn.

She looked beautiful, with her painted eyes and gilded robe, exotic and invincible. But I had seen the fear in her. No amount of glamour could hide it now.

"If you're going to crash our party, at least have something to eat." She waved her hand at the elaborate spread of sumptuous dishes and the courtiers who had filled their plates with food—although none of them were actually eating. They were all watching us.

"Why don't you tell him how the ride ends?" I said. I had a pretty good idea how it did.

"Gloriously!" She winked at me. "An interment in the Valley of the Kings."

Quinn beamed. "See? And you were worried."

"That's a funeral!" I informed him.

At that moment one of the courtiers near the throne collapsed to the ground like a rag doll. No one seemed to care.

"Who was that?" I asked.

Now Quinn looked a bit concerned. "Uh . . . the food taster."

I looked around at the courtiers in attendance, who were still not eating from their plates.

Quinn brought his hand to his stomach. "I don't feel so good." He stumbled back onto his settee. A girl tried to feed him another date, but he pushed her hand away. "Why do I feel so dizzy?"

"The nature of the ride," answered Cassandra.

I tried not to sound as desperate as I felt. "I'll make you a deal: Let my brother go, and I'll stop right here, on the sixth ride."

A chorus of murmurs broke out behind me.

"Sixth ride, sixth ride, sixth ride, sixth ride . . ."

The crowd's whispers dropped into silence, and courtiers were even more attentive than they had been before. They were clearly impressed by how far I'd gotten, and that fact was not lost on Cassandra.

"Self-sacrifice . . . I like it! But why should I bargain now, when I already have you both?"

Quinn fell to his knees, gripping his stomach. "Blake . . . help me."

I lunged toward him, but the guards held me back. Even if I broke free, what could I do?

"You can't save him," Cassandra said. "You couldn't save anyone ten years ago, and you can't save your brother now."

Ten years ago? My anger flared. "*You* caused that accident, not me!"

"But *you* were the one who let them die!"

"That's not true!" It was as if I were shrinking down to be that child again, smashing, smashing, smashing against her accusations, like I smashed against the unyielding emergency exit door. . . .

The angrier I got, the calmer she became. "They died because you didn't try hard enough to open that door."

"I was seven years old!"

Quinn fell over groaning and curled up like a baby. Cassandra was right; I couldn't save Quinn. Maybe I never could. But was it too late for him to save himself?

"There's a way out of every ride, Quinn," I shouted to

him, hoping he was still conscious enough to hear me. "There's a way out of every ride!"

But as the guards dragged me out Cassandra shook her head and said, "Not for the king."

The Egyptians did not have dungeons—at least not in the medieval sense—but they did have plenty of tombs. The place they dumped me was every bit as nasty as one of those medieval dungeons where people got tossed in the Dark Ages and were left there to rot. An *oubliette*, that's the word. It sounds French, but five'll get you ten it was invented by ancient Egyptians.

The guards said nothing as they threw me in. They merely ripped my watch from my wrist, figuring I'd have no further use for it. It was the one thing that had stayed with me from ride to ride, an ever present reminder of the passing night. Then they heaved a heavy stone over the opening, which sealed me in with an echoing boom. It didn't seem like Cassandra to leave me here to die; but perhaps I had her so scared, she just wanted to be rid of me.

I heard something move in the cell just a few feet away from me, and I froze. Instantly my mind ran through all the things it could possibly be. Rats. Cobras. Scorpions.

There was a narrow slit in the roof, not wide enough to climb through but wide enough to bring in a small shaft of light from high above. My eyes adjusted to the light, and I strained to see what nature of creature I'd been entombed with.

It wasn't a creature, but a person. Another prisoner. He was chained to the tomb wall and looked weak, as if he had been in this place for a very long time. Yet he didn't seem surprised to see me.

"Hello, Blake," he said. "Damn, you've grown."

It was like being smashed in the head with a pole again.

"Dad?"

"So here we are," he said. "At least *you* didn't get chained to the wall."

I closed my eyes. This was not possible. It was just another trick of the ride. It had to be. "You're not really here!" I said through gritted teeth. "You're a fake. My real father is somewhere in Oregon with his new family."

"Idaho."

"Shut up!" I opened my eyes again, trying to will the vision away, but it didn't work. If there was anyone in this world I didn't want to see—let alone ride with, it would be him. This man whom I locked out of my mind so long ago. This man whom I barely remembered.

"Are you real?"

"How the hell should I know?"

A whole host of unwanted, unhelpful emotions began to cloud my focus and reasoning. I didn't need this. I had enough to face without facing *him*.

"Too bad. You've got me, whether you want me or not," he said.

"I didn't say anything."

"Didn't you?"

And that told me all I needed to know. He had read

my thoughts, which meant he wasn't real. It was just the park, reading my mind again, throwing out yet another stumbling block to slow me down and keep me distracted until my time ran out. That explained why his face was hidden in shadow. It was because I couldn't really remember his face, and the ride couldn't spit back what my mind couldn't feed it. I knew all this in my head, and yet I also knew it didn't matter that he wasn't real, because there's a part of you that your mind can't reach. It's the part of you that jumps when the monster pops out of the darkness on a movie screen. It's the part that's endlessly amazed by magicians, even though you know their tricks are just sleight of hand. It believes what it sees, and right now it saw my father.

"If you think I'm gonna fight with you or forgive you for abandoning us, forget it. You're not sucking me into some big emotional thing."

"Who says I want to?"

I paced the tomb, stumbling over chunks of stone that littered the ground, angry at myself for feeling angry at all. Someday there'd be a time and place to face my father in the real world. But not here. Not now. I forced myself to stop pacing. I had to bring clarity to my thoughts. "I'm getting out of here."

"This is a tomb," my phantom father said. "It can only be opened from the outside."

I concentrated on the massive sealing stone. *My strength comes from my will.* I hurled myself at the stone and pushed on it with every ounce of determination I had. I pushed and pressed and rammed against it, bruising my shoulders and scraping my hands. The stone didn't budge.

"You never did have much willpower."

"Don't talk to me!" I fell to the ground, crouching in the corner that was farthest away from him.

Time ticked by in silence. All I could hear was my own breathing, then eventually my own heartbeat and the occasional rattle of chains across the tomb as my fellow prisoner shifted positions. Was this eternity for me, then? A cold, claustrophobic hell, with a living reminder of why my life got so screwed up?

A few minutes more, then a sound grated against the silence. The grinding of stone on stone, followed by a sliver of light cutting across the chamber. The heavy stone door opened, and a burly, menacing figure entered with a torch. It only took a moment for me to recognize him. It was the linebacker guard from the hilltop temple—the one whose life I'd spared. The mark from the whip was still there around his oversized neck.

I stood up as he approached. "Is it true what they say?" he asked. "You've really made it through six rides?"

"This is my sixth," I told him.

He smiled like a little kid. "I've never met anyone who's made it that far. There are rumors about you spreading through all the rides." The guard looked up at the small slit in the roof and the distant sliver of blue sky beyond. "Is it still out there?"

"What do you mean?"

"The real world. I keep trying to remember what it was like. Sometimes I can't."

I took a step closer to him. He was real—a rider who got caught in the park at dawn, like the bartender in that tavern. "How long have you been here?"

"I've lost track. There are no days here. The sun never moves in the sky. The clouds never change."

A faint rattle from the corner reminded me that my "father" was still there. I turned, and although I looked directly at him, the glare from the torch had left a dark spot on my retina. I couldn't see his face, and I knew that no matter how hard I tried to see it, I never would. The park couldn't show me what it didn't know. Even so, this phantom father could help me.

"You're not real. You're just another false face of this park, but that means you know things about this place that I don't. So you're going to tell me what I want to know."

He shifted his arms, rattling his chains. "Why would I do that?"

My hands balled into fists, but I crossed my arms to keep myself from using them. "Because somehow you're also my father, and you owe me and Quinn more than you could possibly imagine."

He said nothing to that.

"So you're going to tell me what I want to know," I repeated.

The guard looked from me to him to me again.

"What do you want to know?" my father whispered.

"I want to know about Cassandra. Who is she? *What* is she?"

He sighed and looked down. "She's the tidal wave that

wiped out the Minoans. She's the eruption that leveled Pompeii. Whenever something horrible happens in the world—something senseless—whenever there are no survivors, Cassandra is there."

The magnitude of what he was telling me was as heavy a weight as a pyramid cornerstone, but it was lightened by what I now came to realize.

"What if there was *one* survivor?" I asked.

He said nothing more.

The guard stepped between us. "What are you saying?"

My brain was whirling, but I did my best to explain. "There was an accident a long time ago, and she was there. A school bus spun out of control on an icy road and fell into a deep ravine. I was the only one who survived."

I could feel the guard's excitement build as he considered it. "So then, you were *supposed* to die?"

"But I didn't."

He looked at my "father," who turned his shadowy face toward the stone.

"If no one survives Cassandra, and you did," said the guard, "then you could be the only one who's ever beaten her!"

I shook my head. "I didn't beat her, I just survived."

"So survive again! How did you survive the first time?"

"I don't remember."

"Try! You must remember *something*."

I turned away in frustration. "I've been through it a

thousand times! The bus was spinning out of control. We crashed through the guardrail, and I couldn't open the back door."

"And then?"

"And then *nothing*!" I paced away, but there was nowhere to go in the small chamber. "There was nothing else! One moment I was there at the back of the bus, and the next thing I remember, I was home, and no one was talking about it, and no one has since." I felt like pounding my head against the wall to shake loose the memory. There was a gap in there. I always knew it was there, but since no one ever discussed the crash, it was easy to ignore. The crash had knocked me unconscious. The concussion erased my memory of the trauma, and that was that. Why did it matter? Why should anyone care?

"If you're going to be the one to make it out," said the guard, "you're going to have to remember what you did."

He looked at me for a moment more, then motioned to the open door. "Come on. I can lead you to the seventh ride."

But getting out wasn't enough. "What about my brother?"

"Who?"

"The pharaoh—King Tut."

The guard lowered his eyes. "You can't save him."

He was right about that. Only Quinn could save Quinn. I knew that. But if he was still alive, perhaps I could give him the means to save himself. "Where would he be now? Where would they take him?"

"It doesn't matter," he said flatly. "King Tut dies—King Tut *always* dies. You can't change the ride."

Well, we'd see about that. I started to follow the guard out, but in the corner of the room the phantom image of my father began to speak.

"Blake?"

His face was still fuzzy and unclear, but I had to admit his voice was the voice I remembered.

"I told you what you wanted to know. Now you have to do something for me."

"What?"

"Let me out of here," he said. "Please. I've been in this place for a long, long time."

In the torchlight I could see how truly helpless he was in those shackles. It was a fair request. Whatever he might deserve, I didn't think he deserved this tomb. I picked up a stone lying on the ground and smashed the chains until the links broke.

Once he was free, he left. Simple as that. Just like he did all those years ago. No apologies, no thank-yous, no good-byes. Still, it didn't change the choice I made to let him go.

12

No Guts, No Glory

The room where they had taken Quinn was a long chamber full of stone tables, and you can guess what was on each of those tables. The process of mummification is not pretty. Making one mummy is bad enough, but here, where there was a new King Tut every evening, it was an assembly line—or a disassembly line, I guess you might say. On each table was another unfortunate rider in some stage of the process. Quinn was in the earliest stage, and still, to my relief, very much alive.

The temple guard and a few of his conspirators had smuggled me in, but in my current hiding place I couldn't do anything to help my brother. Not yet, anyway. He was just a few yards away from me, but all I could do was watch. He was still groggy from the drugs he'd been given, but even if he'd had all his strength, he wouldn't have been able to tear free from the ropes that tied down his arms and legs. He glanced at the fully wrapped mummy on the slab next to him.

An old woman with red cheeks tended to him. She seemed pleasant enough, humming to herself as she removed Quinn's facial rings, and put them on an alabaster tray.

"Who said you could take those?" Quinn said, defiant to the last.

"You just relax, dearie," she said, sounding like someone's grandma. "I'll take care of everything." She smiled at him and gently patted his hand. He pulled his hand away.

"So am I dead now?" Quinn asked. "Is this what death is?"

"No, you're just drugged. In this heat it's always best to keep you alive until we begin work, there being no refrigeration and all."

Quinn thought about this while Madame Embalmer continued humming to herself, measuring Quinn with some sort of ruler shorter than a yardstick. Maybe it was a cubit stick.

"What are you doing?" Quinn asked.

"Measuring you for your sarcophagus, dearie." She turned and shouted angrily at one of her assistants. "ACHMED!" she yelled. "Easy on the salt!"

Her gawky assistant, who didn't look much older than me, had shoveled a mountain of sea salt over an ex-Tut who was already well on the way to long-term preservation. "Yes, ma'am," Achmed said dutifully.

Madame Embalmer shook her head and looked down at Quinn. "Waste, waste, waste! The way he uses that salt, you'd think the Dead Sea were around the corner!"

That's when Cassandra showed up, still decked out in her Egyptian glory. I flinched and then realized that even a flinch could give me away. But I was lucky. No one saw me.

She looked at Quinn and kissed him on the forehead. "I want him put on the fast track," she told Madame Embalmer.

"Was he a good Tut?" she asked.

"Oh, completely incompetent," Cassandra said.

I could see Quinn's eyes getting moist, but his jaw was still set hard. I wonder what he was feeling. Shame? Humiliation? The realization that this truly was the end of the line? Suddenly he pulled against his bonds, but Madame Embalmer was right there to comfort him.

"There, there. Don't you worry."

"Wh-What's going to happen to me?"

The old woman looked at Cassandra for permission before speaking.

"Well, it's really rather simple," said Madame Embalmer, taking on a singsong tone of voice, as if she were reading him a bedtime story. "First we disembowel—"

"Disembowel?"

"Yes. We take out your heart, lungs, liver, kidneys—every organ—and tuck them nicely away in their own little jars. Except, of course, for your brain. We pull *that* out through your nose with a hook."

Quinn whimpered.

"Then," continued the old woman, "when you're nice and empty on the inside, we cover you with salt, to dry you up." At the sound of a nasty *splat,* she turned to her assistant.

"ACHMED!"

Achmed picked up something from the floor and fumbled with it in his arms. I couldn't quite make out what it was, but it looked suspiciously liverlike. "Sorry, ma'am."

"Butterfingers!"

Achmed slipped the thing carefully into an earthen jar with a sickening slosh. I closed my eyes and grimaced. Now I had a legitimate reason never to eat my mother's liver-and-onions again.

There were tears rolling down Quinn's cheeks. He was afraid, and maybe for the first time in his life he was admitting that he was. "I don't want to be empty on the inside," he cried. "Please . . . please don't do this."

For a moment I thought I saw compassion in Cassandra's gaze, but it only lasted for a moment. "Shut him up," she said. "I don't like it."

"I'll go get a gag for him."

The old woman left, and Cassandra strode down to the far end of the hall, where the mummies could no longer talk back.

This was my chance. I rose from the table where I'd been lying and hurried to Quinn. When he saw me, his eyes bulged, and he opened his mouth to scream. I clamped my linen-covered hand over his mouth before he could make a sound.

"Be quiet, it's me!" I peeled the mummy wrappings from my head.

"Blake?"

"No, Ramses the Great."

The temple guard had done a good job of wrapping me up, and we'd gathered enough workers to carry me here and quietly leave me on the table. Of course, getting out wouldn't be as easy as getting in.

There was a knife strapped to my arm. I pulled it out and used it to cut the bonds on Quinn's right hand. I was about to cut the other ropes but stopped. Instead, I put the knife into his free hand. He had to do it. I couldn't do it for him. He had to choose, or we'd just be right back here again tomorrow, or the next day, or the next.

He looked at me almost as if he could hear what I was thinking, then he sliced through the rest of the ropes. "I'm done with this place," he whispered. "I wanna take my organs and go home."

He hopped off the table, but as we were about to slip away he suddenly stopped.

"Come on! What are you waiting for?"

He stared at the tray beside the table—the one that held all of his facial rings. It was like his whole life was on that little tray: his alienation and his anger, his auto-destruct attitude.

A few tables away, Achmed had spotted us.

Quinn hesitated a moment more, then reached for the tray, picking out a single ring. A little diamond stud. It was the one that Carl, Mom's fiancé, had given him. He fixed it in his ear as we ran.

"No! Stop them!" Cassandra ran at us from the far end of the room. Workers grabbed for us, but their hands were slick from the oily balms of mummification. We evaded their grasps, but Cassandra was much faster than we were. She was almost upon us when Achmed came out from behind a table and hurled a shovelful of salt into her eyes.

"Go on! Get to the seventh ride!" he shouted. We raced out without looking back.

We met up with the temple guard at the outer gate of the palace. Racing down the steps, we caught the attention of guards and slaves, courtiers and warriors. I expected them to try to stop us. After all, part of their jobs was to make sure the ride went smoothly. Instead, I heard murmurs spreading through the crowd as we ran past.

"That's him!"

"There he is!"

"His sixth ride!"

Something was stirring in these people that hadn't been here before: a sense of hope! Now taskmasters broke the chains of slaves, artisans abandoned their work, and a great rumbling began to fill the earth and sky. As I looked up at the mottled heavens the sky began to melt, like wax in a furnace.

"What's happening?"

"I'm not sure," the guard said. "I think the ride's breaking down!"

"What?" said Quinn. But I understood, and I understood why. It's not walls that make a prison, but the willingness of the prisoners. These rides were built on the broken, resigned spirits of those trapped here; but without them, the rides couldn't hold.

One more ride, I told myself. "We have to get to the next ride before this one crashes!"

"This way!" said the guard.

"No, this way's faster," I heard a voice behind me say. "I'll show you!" It was the street vendor. He tossed aside his tray of trinkets and led us through a narrow alley, pointing as we came out the other side. "There."

It was the Great Pyramid of Cheops, its golden tip glowing against the melting sky. There was a hieroglyph emblazoned on the golden tip, but it wasn't Egyptian: It was the ride symbol, shining a neon red. To reach it, we'd have to climb the pyramid.

Quinn and I took off across the sands toward the pyramid in the distance, and as I looked around me I realized we were not alone. Dozens ran alongside of us now, a wave of people escorting us, cheering me on to the last ride.

I knew Cassandra was somewhere nearby. I could feel the wild extremes of her soul—the searing heat, the frosty cold. But the wake of excitement created by the ride in revolt protected us and swept us toward the pyramid.

The rumble in the earth grew more violent, and now the entire sky was melting away. Then, as we reached the base of the pyramid, the ground tore open beneath me. Quinn was already up on the first stone block, but I lost my footing and tumbled into the widening crevasse. Sand poured in all around me; steam rose from down below as I fell. I was so close! So close! My hands had touched the pyramid, but I hadn't moved fast enough.

Now my eyes were so full of sand and steam, I couldn't see where I was falling, but I didn't have to see; I knew. I knew because of the sounds around me. The terrible gnashing sounds of gears.

I'd fallen into The Works.

13
The Works

I may forget everything else that happened to me in the park. The memories of the rides may be sucked from my mind by a real world that cannot allow such things to exist. But I will never forget The Works. That will live on in my nightmares. I will feel its grinding metallic teeth every time I see scenes of war, or a plane crash, or some other disaster on the news, too terrible to watch but too riveting to look away from. I will see in those things the dark clockwork that gets built gear by gear out of our dying dreams and our desperate fears. Cassandra did not build The Works. We're the ones who built it. She just gave it form. I know that as surely as I know that I stood there, and watched the wheels turn.

I fell through the crack in the desert sands and landed with a clang on an iron catwalk in a place so hot and humid, my lungs felt as if I were breathing water. All around me were gears, shiny chrome gears, from the size of a dime to what seemed the size of planets. They all revolved at a fever pitch, turning crankshafts and pumping pistons in an unrelenting dance that extended downward into a bottomless pit. The chrome cogs were as cold as a glacier, and yet the air burned furnace-hot. Waves of heat and spatial distortion pulsed out from the great machine, and I had to hold on to the catwalk to overcome a light-headed vertigo as I looked down into the depths. Yet that wasn't the worst of it.

I'd thought at first that whoever was consigned to The Works got ground up in its unforgiving gears like human hamburger, but I was wrong.

There were figures working the machine—hundreds upon hundreds of them. They held levers, valves, and cranks, pushing and pulling in a backbreaking rhythm, but they weren't really holding the machinery. They were *growing* out of it, their flesh melding into the metal of the gear-work, as much a part of the machine as the cogs, pinions, and rotors. Their muscles bulged, sinewy and strong from the work, but their eyes were vacant and reflective chrome.

The park had absorbed them, as Cassandra had said, but I could never have imagined this.

Closest to me were two figures laboring on alternate sides of a two-man pump—a seesaw device, like an old-fashioned hand-cranked railroad car. They struggled to turn a ratchet wheel that was connected to a larger wheel that turned a shaft running down to the sweltering depths. Their eyes—their souls—had been voided into mechanical numbness.

It was Maggie and Russ.

"They make a nice team," I heard Cassandra say.

I turned but couldn't find her. Her voice seemed to come from all around me.

"We're all part of something larger than ourselves," she said. "That's the nature of the universe. And now your friends are part of my machine."

My revulsion and anger fused into something so heavy, I couldn't move. There was nowhere to go. The catwalk ended just behind me at a huge wheel that slowly churned the steam. On either side of the wheel was a drop down into the hellish Works.

Cassandra appeared out of the steam on the narrow catwalk, still adorned in Egyptian splendor. This was it. She was coming in for the final kill. She'd won.

What she said next caught me completely by surprise.

"Thank you, Blake." Her voice was soft yet surprisingly clear over the throbbing of the great machine. "Because of you, I've experienced fear for the first time. Your challenge was remarkable." She put her hands on my shoulders. Something about her touch made the atmosphere of The Works different. Sweat still poured from me, yet I felt chilled deep inside. "You wanted to make a deal before," she said. "Will you deal with me now?"

And against all my better judgment, I said, "What do you have in mind?"

"Stop now," she said, "and you can share it with me."

"Share what?"

"Everything. All the rides and any other ride you can imagine."

"As your slave."

"No, as my equal."

I realized that she was not just holding me, I was holding her as well. Why? If I felt such fury and such revulsion at what she was, why did I hold her? Was it just her beauty that captivated me, or something more?

"This place has always been out of balance," she said. "It was all that I knew. Now I want to experience the balance you bring."

Suddenly the slave rags I wore began to shimmer like gold. Jewels grew in the fabric, and I found myself clad in a robe of rubies, sapphires, and emeralds.

"You could be the god Osiris over a new, better Egypt," she told me. "You could build any world you desire, be its king or its subject; you could experience thrills or tranquility and move freely from one ride to another, just as I do." She ran her hands down the length of my jewel-covered arms, then clasped my hands in hers. "I am the park's soul. I want *you* to be its mind."

Was she sincere, or was it just another trick? I'd become aware enough to see through her deceptions, and this offer felt real. I had brought her something she never had. I was the only one who ever had.

I tore myself away from her eyes long enough to look at Russ and Maggie, laboring across the chasm. "What about them? What about my brother? Will you let them go?"

"I can't do that. But if you stay here, we'll create rides for each of them. They can have whatever they want, whatever they need, forever and ever."

Could that be possible? Would she really put that kind of power in my hands? I imagined the rides I might design for my friends. For Maggie I'd build a palace of mirrors that told all the truths about herself that were worth telling. How she was kind, generous, compassionate, and, yes, beautiful. Maybe a log flume for Russ! Not a slow, dull one, but one where he could ride down the rapids of an endless river, camping every night at its bank. And for my brother, perhaps a parachute jump that air-dropped food to a starving people. It would open him up to the thrill found in giving, rather than taking.

"Think about it, Blake. This place could be different with you here."

The more I thought about Cassandra's offer, the more appealing it got. I tried to weigh my alternatives against each other. If I took one more ride and survived it, I'd win my freedom. But if I ended my journey here, I'd win the park. A master of worlds . . . it was a dizzying thought. It wasn't the power, but the peace that appealed to me—the peace of truly being in control at last. She was right: The park would be different with me sharing the power. And *she* would be different if we weren't cast as enemies.

"The larger the park grows, the more real it becomes," she said. "In time your world will become the false one, and all these worlds will be real. Come build them with me."

It was there that the bubble burst.

"Build them how? Build them on the spirits of others you'll trap here?"

She answered me with no shame or remorse. "Nothing comes without a price, and no one comes who doesn't choose to be here."

I looked around me once more. So many were trapped here—not just the ones in The Works, but those forced to playact in the worlds of each ride. All for her amusement. If I took my place with Cassandra here, it would be for *my* amusement as well. I suppose we can all be accused of using people in our lives, but I could never use people the way she did.

"I've given you your first real challenge," I told her, "and now you know what it means to be afraid. But there's something else you still need to experience."

"And what's that?"

"You need to lose."

I reached back, grasping firmly on to the largest wheel, which looked eerily like a giant Ferris wheel. As it turned it tore me out of her arms, lifting me up and up.

I heard her scream in anger, but in a moment her voice disappeared into the grinding of The Works, and she was hidden by the billowing plumes of steam.

As the wheel took me higher the jewels on my robe dropped away and disappeared into the gear-work. Would I have been a decent "god"? Perhaps. At least I'd like to think so. But the cost of accepting the job was too great.

Now my clothes were just rags again as I rode the wheel to the uppermost level of The Works. There, the machinery gave way to a fissure, still streaming sand from Egypt up above. I jumped from the wheel to the jagged rocks, sliding and scrambling for a foothold, kicking rocks down into the depths, until I finally had a grip and stopped sliding. Then I shoved my fingertips and toes into cracks in the stone, pulling my way up. I wasn't much of a rock climber, but I was learning fast.

Quinn saw me the second I came up through the mist. He must have been waiting there all this time. He never lost hope in me. He reached down and helped me out.

"I thought it was over," he said. "I thought you were gone for sure!"

"And miss the next ride?" I looked toward the top of the Great Pyramid where the ride symbol glowed. It reminded me that I hadn't kept my soul, not yet. Refusing Cassandra's deal bought me nothing if I didn't get to the next ride, and getting there wouldn't be easy. The pyramid stones we had to climb were like six-foot-high steps, and there were dozens of them.

"We'll help each other up each step," I told Quinn. "First you, then me." I gave Quinn a boost up to the next ledge.

We climbed one immense stone after another. Above us the blue sky melted away. Below us the voices of the crowd that had gathered to cheer us became fainter and more distant. Finally we reached the illuminatus, the golden tip of the pyramid. The ride symbol glowed a searing white, matching the glowing brand on the backs of our hands. The spiral of the symbol spanned ten feet, and in the very center of the symbol, where the wave intersected the spiral, was a button about the size of my hand. I slammed my palm down on the button, forcing it in until a mechanism clicked. Somewhere deep down in The Works, a new gear engaged.

Nothing happened at first. Everything seemed to hang in silence, waiting. Then something began to move. I heard the scraping of stone against stone, and just beneath the golden tip of the pyramid a row of panels fell away. Thick iron spokes extended outward just below us, and the entire tip of the pyramid began to rotate.

"Hold on!" I yelled to Quinn. There wasn't much to hold on to, but we clung to the face of the golden illuminatus as it gained speed, rotating faster and faster.

Eight iron spokes had grown from beneath the pyramid tip, like the eight legs of a spider. From the end of each spoke a pair of pods appeared that revolved around each other. It was the Tilt-A-Whirl I'd seen when I first entered the park. The little pairs of pods spun and dipped, weaving in and out of one another like the blades of an eggbeater.

"We have to get into one of those pods!" I shouted over the thrumming of the ride.

"They're too far away!" Quinn shouted back. "We'll never make it!"

"Who hung fifty feet over Six Flags to get his stupid hat? Come on!" I pulled him off the golden face of the pyramid tip, and we dropped onto a black iron arm of the spinning ride.

We had to get to the end of the arm and drop into one of the spinning pods. But as we shimmied farther out on the stem, centrifugal force threatened to hurl us off. I turned around and eased my way toward the end of the spoke feet first, hugging the cold metal as tightly as I could. Quinn did the same, and we inched our way out, the world spinning madly around us. The desert was a blur below us. There was nothing else in the world now but me, Quinn, and the ride.

I felt the pulses of wind from the two spinning pods at the end of the spoke and heard the *whoosh-whoosh-whoosh* as they beat past, sounding like the blades of a propeller. They chased each other in circles, hanging beneath the arm to which we clung.

Now the ride wasn't just spinning, it was wobbling as well, like an off-balance top, making me feel drunk and giddy.

Whoosh-whoosh-whoosh.

The only way to make it into one of the pods below was to jump. If we jumped a second too late, we'd fall to our deaths. If we jumped a second too soon, we'd be hit by a pod and squashed like bugs on a windshield.

Timing was everything. I tried to match my breathing to the spinning of the pods, locking my vision in one place, ignoring the vertigo, and concentrating on the jump.

Whoosh-whoosh-whoosh.

"We're gonna die!" wailed Quinn. "Oh, God, we're gonna die!"

"Shut up! You sound like me!"

Even as I overcame my fears, terror had attacked Quinn with a vengeance. It was so foreign to him that he didn't know how to control it. It practically paralyzed him. I knew I'd have to jump first, then talk him down. I took one more moment to estimate the length of the fall. I'd only get one shot at this.

I jumped and instantly panicked. I was falling too far. I had missed. . . . But then my view of the pyramid base below was eclipsed by the pod, and I landed inside.

Up above, Quinn still clung to the arm of the ride, his cheek firmly pressed against the cold steel like a gecko clinging to a branch.

"Jump!"

"It's too fast!"

"Just jump!"

"I'll fall!"

"You can make it!"

He locked his eyes on the spinning pod, let loose a battle cry, and sprang from the arm of the ride. He missed the pod. His body slid down its slick black hull, but his arm caught the edge like a hanger hook. I grabbed him by his arm, but I lost my grip. Then I got a grip on his hair, holding it just long enough to grab his shirt with my other hand. It began to tear, but by then I had hooked a finger in a loop on the back of his jeans. He grabbed the edge of the pod and finally flipped himself in.

"Are we done?" he asked. "Can we go home now?"

Now that we were inside the pod, it began to change, as I knew it would. I felt the fracturing of metal as our pod tore free from the ride, but we didn't fall. We soared. The nose of the pod elongated. A dome grew over our heads, and the cabin expanded. An instrument panel sprang out in front of us as our little bench divided, becoming two separate seats, molded to fit the contours of our bodies. The instrument panel looked nothing like that of the Japanese Zero. The entire thing was a computer screen filled with holographic buttons and gauges that all seemed to be labeled in some language like Pig Klingon.

"I know this!" said Quinn. "This is the spaceship on the cover of a CD I have—*Nuclear Galaxy's Greatest Hits!*"

"Great. How do you fly it?"

"I don't know. All I know is that there's also a picture of the ship blowing up on the back cover."

I looked up from the strange control panel to the view-port that stretched not only in front of us, but over our heads as well, giving us a 360-degree view. The sky was dark violet, sparking with electricity; and there were clouds, although they really didn't look like clouds. They looked more like tangled, leathery tree limbs, stretching in an endless purple web all around us. Electrical impulses shot along the knotted, ropelike clouds into the violet distance.

"It looks like a nebula," I told Quinn. "A space cloud."

He looked at me sharply. "I know what a nebula is." Then he saw something that shut his attitude down cold. "Bad news!"

I stared ahead. A massive object was hurtling directly at us. It was a moment before I recognized what it was.

"If we're in space," asked Quinn, "what's *that* doing here?"

"I have no idea."

14
Brain-Jam

There's a travel poster of Italy in my room at home, right over my bed. You don't have to see it to know what's on it. There's the Coliseum, the Leaning Tower of Pisa, and that pink place in Venice with all the pigeons—you'd know it if you saw it. Like I've said, I've always dreamed of going to those places and seeing all those things . . . but I never expected to see the Tower of Pisa spinning end over end like a giant tomahawk, heading straight for me.

"Do something!" shouted Quinn.

I looked down at the spaceship's complex computer interface. No mouse, no keypad. I didn't know what to do, but the second I moved my hand close to the interface, a steering column grew up from the screen, into my hand.

"Cool," said Quinn, more relieved than impressed.

My fingers clasped the control stick, and I pulled to the right. An engine fired, and our little space pod veered right, narrowly missing the tumbling stone tower. Now, with the tower gone, I could see that the

space around us was more than just a nebula. It was a
debris field—but this was not exactly your typical space
debris. As we shot forward, unable to slow down, the
Eiffel Tower tumbled by, cutting diagonally across our
path, its movement eerily graceful. Easter Island heads
floated by, their mysterious faces seeming to grin mock-
ingly in the strange lavender light.

I looked beyond the debris to the purple nebula
around us. Something struck me about the way the electrical impulses shot down the web of snaking, intertwin-
ing ropes. It was familiar . . . like something I'd learned
in biology. . . .

And suddenly I knew what this place was supposed
to be.

"I don't think we're in space," I told Quinn.

"Then where are we?"

I sighed. "We're . . . inside my head."

"Oh." Quinn didn't look surprised. "Why do you
have all this crap floating around in your head?"

"If I knew, it wouldn't be there." I was sure if we ric-
ocheted around long enough, we'd find every thought
I'd ever had, transmuted into rock-solid form. Mental
toe-jam. This place was what Cassandra saw when she
looked at me.

I go places sometimes.

Yeah, well, I never thought I'd find myself here.

"I saw this movie once," Quinn said. "A bunch of scientists got shrunk and injected into a guy's blood. They
had to crawl out over his eyeball."

"I don't think it'll be that easy."

A farmhouse tumbled past, colored in sepia tones. A young girl who looked suspiciously like Judy Garland peered out of the window, astonished.

I turned to Quinn. "If you say, 'I don't think we're in Kansas anymore,' I'll smack you."

"Watch out!"

I pulled up, but not fast enough, and we were clipped by Big Ben—the clock that usually chimes out over London but was now revolving in front of us like a pinwheel. The impact sent us spinning, knocking Quinn out of his chair. He bounced weightlessly around the cabin. What bothered me even more than being hit, though, was what I saw on Big Ben's massive clock face. Its hands read ten minutes to six. Ten minutes to dawn. Ten minutes to beat this ride, or it was all over.

I pushed and tugged on the control stick, which fired retros and boosters until I'd straightened us out. I had no idea what direction we faced, but then, every direction was the same in this place. There was no up or down, no left or right.

"Can't you drive safe?" Quinn pulled himself back down into his seat and struggled with a seat-belt harness that looked like it was meant for a creature with three arms.

We smashed into a grafitti-covered subway car, but it sustained most of the damage from the collision, spinning away from us to reveal another spaceship behind it, which jetted out like a cop car at a speed trap. It was sleek and bronze, with curves that were almost feminine, and it took off after us, shooting some sort of multicolored laser weapon. My brain didn't have to fire too many synaptic sparks to figure out who piloted that ship.

The blast tore a hole in our left wing—a hole that sizzled with every color of the spectrum.

"It's an Aurora-Refractive Laser Cannon," said Quinn. "Straight out of my *Steroid Avenger* comic books."

Cassandra didn't try to contact us. I suppose she had nothing left to say to me beyond the constant blasts from her weapon. Another blast caught our right flank, jolting us badly, but we held together.

"Check the controls," I told Quinn. "If she has an Aurora-Refractive whatever, then maybe we have one too!"

He scanned the unreadable control panel, then did a quick eenie-meenie-meinie-mo and touched one of the virtual buttons.

A blast shield came down over the dome, completely shutting out our view. We were flying blind.

"Oops."

He quickly hit the button again, and the blast shield lifted to reveal something huge, smooth, and silver filling our entire view. Quinn got the big picture before I did.

"The *Hindenburg*!"

I pulled up, feeling the g-forces pressing me deep into my seat. We came within inches of hitting the giant airship.

"Why, of all things, is the *Hindenburg* here?" I searched my memory, but couldn't find a reason for *that* to be in my own personal brain-jam.

"It's on my Led Zep poster," Quinn said. "In case you haven't noticed, this is *my* ride too." Now Quinn randomly hit buttons on the control panel looking for weapons. Lights came on and off; the chairs reclined. Finally a multicolored laser blast shot out of the nose of our ship and blew Jefferson's face from Mount Rushmore.

"Got it!"

"Great! Now figure out how to aim it."

He looked at me like I'd asked him to perform open heart surgery.

"Never mind. Just blow up stuff in our way."

"I can do that." He concentrated all his attention on the debris field, with his finger paused above the button.

I pulled sharply to the right, trying to dodge Cassandra's blasts, but she scored a direct hit. Part of our dome bubbled and singed, but it didn't rupture.

She knows me! I thought. *She knows every move I'll make and every direction I'll turn.* I was too predictable. If I was going to pilot us through this, I had to fight every natural tendency I had. To outsmart Cassandra, I needed to become a master of wild, unpredictable behavior. Which meant . . .

"Quinn, I need your help."

"You've got a plan?"

"My plan is not to have a plan. That's why I need your help."

"You want me to fly, then?"

But that wouldn't work either. Cassandra would know right away. She'd be able to predict Quinn's moves as well as mine. The only way to outsmart her was to outsmart ourselves. So I told Quinn, "We have to somehow do it together."

I scanned the sky ahead of us.

"What are you looking for?"

"Something big to hide behind."

"No," said Quinn. "Look for something small. We can knock it into her path."

"What if we knock something *big* into her path?"

"If it's too big, we could blow up when we hit it."

I smiled. She wouldn't expect that we'd risk that! We came around to see the Arc de Triomphe floating in our path in a slow off-center revolution. I turned toward it.

"We're crazy, you know?" said Quinn. I had to agree. And, you know, it felt good.

We smashed into the huge stone arch, sending it spinning away from us. It crushed our nose flat, but it also spun right into Cassandra's ship, which tumbled wildly off course. Her ship looked almost as dented as ours. In a few moments she had her vehicle under control again—but for once we were on the offensive.

"Blow it out of the sky!" Quinn said.

That was my first instinct too, but it would be too obvious. She'd have some sort of shield against a direct attack. Instead, I singled out the nearest obstacle: the Statue of Liberty. Perhaps Miss Liberty would buy our freedom.

Quinn fired. Miss Liberty detonated, sending a rain of green-copper shrapnel into Cassandra's path. She hit the shrapnel field, and one of her engines began to smoke.

"I've got an idea," said Quinn. "Bring us around and head back for the *Hindenburg*, but don't make it obvious."

Quinn had trusted me, so now I put my trust in him. I maneuvered in a wide arc, bobbing in and out of debris, making it appear that I was just trying to evade Cassandra's blasts. The airship was the largest piece of debris in this brain-junkyard, and it wasn't hard to find again.

"Fly like we're going around it," said Quinn. "Like we're going to hide behind it."

"We'll let her think she's catching up to us and—"

I didn't have to say the rest, because we both knew. Quinn and I were connected now, like we were when we were younger, when our differences didn't pull us apart, but made us complete.

Quinn looked behind us, keeping his eyes on Cassandra's ship, letting me know her position second by second. We bobbed and wove closer to the behemoth of an airship, its taught silver fabric a pale lavender, reflecting the sparking violet heavens. As we rounded its belly Cassandra was right on our tail. Then suddenly I pulled up, tearing though the fabric of the airship, smashing through its support girders. The hydrogen gas ignited, and for an instant flames tried to engulf us, but then we came through the other side. Cassandra's ship got caught right in the heart of the blast. I brought us around to watch as flames consumed the *Hindenburg*. As the airship burned down to its aluminum skeleton, Cassandra's crippled ship fell away from the wreckage, charred and smoking.

Quinn kept his hand near the weapon controls. "She could be faking. . . ."

So we watched. We saw an engine try to fire, then go dark. She was completely disabled, and although I'm sure she knew her way out of this ride, she could no longer attack us.

It should have been enough, but it wasn't. *Besting* her was not enough. We had to beat her—and that meant getting out of the ride. I took us away from the flaming ruins of the airship and sped toward open space. Before us a series of smaller objects dotted the sparking sky— hundreds of them, maybe thousands. It took a moment for me to realize what they were, and when I did, my heart sank. It was a minefield . . . of sorts.

"Are those . . . cars?" Quinn asked.

I nodded. "Not just any old cars. They're Pintos. Every last one of them."

It was a field of floating automobiles that stretched as far as the eye could see, and it was so dense, you couldn't even see beyond it.

"How hard do you have to ram a Pinto to make it blow up?" Quinn asked.

"I'm sure that here, they blow up on impact. And how much you wanna bet the only way out is on the other side?" I scanned the minefield, then turned to Quinn. "Okay, what would you do?"

"I'd try to weave through them."

"And I'd try to go around them." I knew neither strategy would work. Going around would take too long, and weaving through, well, I wasn't *that* good of a pilot. I took a deep breath and prepared myself for a third choice. "Close the blast shield."

"What? We won't be able to see!"

"Exactly."

"What are you gonna do? Fly by Braille?"

"Kind of."

"Should I trust you?"

"Probably not."

But he did anyway. He lowered the blast shield as we approached the field. "I never thought you'd want to go out like this," he said.

"I don't intend to."

I knew these worlds well enough now to know that their strength came from our weaknesses. The park tapped into our longings, our fears, our habits, and our choices. This minefield had been perfectly, strategically placed to cause the most damage if Quinn and I followed our normal patterns of behavior when we encountered it. So much of my life had been under tight control. So much of Quinn's life had been wild insanity. What we needed now was both: a directed burst of controlled insanity.

I gunned the engine, then took my hand off the controls, letting the ship fly a blind beeline through the minefield.

We hit the first Pinto. It dented our hull. I heard the

car blow up, but we were moving so fast, it blew up behind us. Another one hit our underbelly, jarring me through the seat of my pants, but again, it exploded behind us.

Impact after impact, explosion after explosion. Smoke clouded the cabin from a fire in the engines.

"This ship's not going to last much longer," Quinn said.

"It doesn't have to. It's just got to last a few more seconds."

One more mine bashed in our entire left side, but the hull held its integrity, and I closed my eyes, waiting for the next one—the one that would do us in.

It never came. Nothing more hit us. The only sounds now were the crackling of flames at the back of the cabin and the sizzle of frying technology.

Quinn looked at me, then opened the blast shield. It labored open to reveal a new sight dead ahead. The minefield and all of its debris were behind us. A spiral pattern of stars slowly revolved in front of us. It was the most beautiful thing I'd ever seen.

"Is that a galaxy?" asked Quinn.

I smiled. "It looks like a turnstile to me."

Our engines were gone, our ship was burning up, but the cosmic turnstile pulled us in faster and faster toward its center. Acceleration pressed me back against the chair.

Then I did something I'd never done before. I put my hands up in the air. Way up, like you're supposed to do on the fastest, wildest roller coasters. I looked to Quinn and grinned. He nodded and put his hands up in the air as well as we shot through the center of the swirling turnstile galaxy—one last thrill for both of us to share, in absolute defiance of the ride.

I think that was the moment I really found my brother.

15
Tilt

We skidded to a stop on a barren landscape—a cold, gray no-man's-land beneath a black, dead sky. We climbed out of our pod, which was no longer a ship, just a small Tilt-A-Whirl ride pod, dented and lopsided, but otherwise not much different from how it started. Snaking fingers of ground fog streaked the cratered ground, and the air held a stale, caustic odor like the smell of a junkyard refrigerator.

"What is this place?" Quinn asked.

Dozens of poles poked out of the ground, and at the end of each pole was a sign. ONE WAY. DO NOT ENTER. STOP. YIELD. NO U-TURN. They all pointed in different directions, like they were just standing around, not sure what, or whom, to direct.

A pale clock face hung in the sky like the soulless face of a winter moon. The clock showed 6:00 A.M., but when I looked closer, I could see that the second hand showed twelve seconds to the hour, and I watched those last seconds tick away.

We'd made it through all seven rides in time.

So why weren't we out?

"Cassandra!" I called out to the black sky. "I did it, Cassandra. I made all seven rides. By your own rules you have to let me out!"

No answer.

"You have to let me out!"

Then she appeared out of the fog, weaving through the forest of road signs. She was definitely worse for the wear. The copper sheen to her hair was gone; it was almost ashen gray. Her face was pale and world-weary, like a young woman old before her time. Her gown was moth-torn silk, like an old shroud, and its color, like the stuffed bear she first handed me, was what you get when you mix all your paints together.

Now I understood the threat I posed and why Cassandra was so frightened. With each ride, I grew stronger, while she—and the park itself—grew weaker. Because of me, her magic was faltering. I doubt even she knew what would happen if it failed completely.

"Six A.M.," I said. "Time to let me go."

"Yes," she said, her voice raspy. "I said I'd let you go, and I will." She sounded far too calm. It troubled me. "*You* get to go home. But Quinn goes to The Works."

"What?"

"He only made it through five rides."

I looked at Quinn, who was turning as white as the clock looming in the sky.

"You've made the rides unstable," Cassandra said. "There's lots of damage to repair, and I need every soul on the job. I've got a nice place for Quinn next to Maggie and Russ."

I shook my head, refusing to believe it. "That's not fair!"

"Life's not fair," she snapped. "Who said eternity has to be?"

"I won't go without him!"

"I'll make you go. I'll put you outside the gate, and for the rest of your life you'll know that you left your brother and friends behind. Unless . . ."

"Unless what?"

Cassandra took her time answering me. "Tell you what. I'll give you one chance to earn their freedom."

She was playing games again, taunting, teasing. She dangled their freedom in front of me like a carrot, and I had no choice but to reach for it.

"What do I have to do?"

"All you have to do is take one more ride. . . ."

She gestured toward a dark patch of ground; but it wasn't just ground. It was moving. It was a large turntable of dark gray asphalt, about fifty yards in diameter. It slowly revolved, and out of the misty darkness spun an object: a single teacup, just large enough for a person to sit in. A spinning teacup ride. That's all. It might not have been so bad, except for one thing:

The teacup was yellow.

School bus yellow.

"Take this final ride, and if you make it through, your brother and your friends get to go home with you."

The yellow teacup revolved back into the misty darkness.

"You don't have to do it," said Quinn. But he was wrong. Even if his fate didn't hang in the balance, I had to take this ride. I turned to Cassandra. "What happens if I don't make it through?"

She only smiled, pulling her hair back from her face.

I took a step toward the slowly revolving patch of asphalt, but Quinn grabbed my arm. "I'll come with you."

"You can't. I ride this one alone."

His eyes grew moist. "Promise me you'll be back," he said. "Promise me you won't disappear."

But I wouldn't make him a promise I might not be able to keep.

Cassandra crossed her arms impatiently. "Are you riding or not?"

I stepped up to the edge of the asphalt turntable. Its surface was slick, with a fine layer of black ice.

"Hey, Blake?"

I turned back to Quinn before I took that step onto the turntable. "Yeah?"

He hesitated. "I'm just wondering . . . did I ever tell you that I love you?"

"No," I answered. "You never did."

He shrugged. "So maybe I will someday."

"Yeah," I said. "Me too."

Then I stepped onto the turntable, and it carried me away from him. "Back in five." I kept my eyes on my brother until he faded into the mist. I turned to see the teacup just a few yards away. I pulled open the cup's little yellow door. The seats inside were dark green leatherette. The wheel in the center was a steering wheel. I closed the door, took my seat, and grabbed the wheel. The teacup began to spin, slowly at first, but picking up speed as I pulled on the wheel, putting my weight behind it. I made that yellow teacup spin faster and faster until everything blurred. The sound of squealing tires began to fill my ears, and suddenly I was—

—*spinning out of control.*

A doomed school bus on an icy day.

Green sticky seats and the smell of cherry bubble gum and a dozen kids screaming as the bus spins round and round and round. Andy Burke, my best friend, falls from his seat to the ground.

I am seven. I am there. This is not just a ride, I am there!

A teacher wails, "Oh my God, oh my God, oh my God."

Mrs. Greer. I remember her name now. I grip on to the seat in front of me to keep from being hurled across the bus. My backpack flies and I never see it again.

My fingers slip from the seat back, and I tumble into the aisle, my cheek hitting the cold black floor that smells of rubber and mud.

"Hold on, Blake!" Mrs. Greer yells.

When I look up, I'm staring straight at the emergency exit at the back of the bus. It seems a hundred yards away.

BAM! We hit something hard, tearing metal. A guardrail flies up from the road, like a piece of confetti. It smashes a window and tumbles away. We've broken through the guardrail at the edge of Colfax Ravine. I know this place. The cliff is steep and rocky. I used to throw paper airplanes from this cliff and never see them hit the bottom. As far as I know, Colfax Ravine is as deep as the Grand Canyon.

The front end of the bus slips over the edge of the cliff, and now the sight of the rear emergency exit door fills my mind, and I scramble toward it. No one else is opening that door. Don't they know—don't they see why that door is there? If no one else will open it, I will!

The bus tilts, its back end lifting into the air. The floor of the bus rises before me like a black wave. I climb the steep angle of the floor to get to the emergency exit at the back. Screams and scraping metal. The smell of pee. Somebody's wet themselves. Maybe it's me.

I reach the back of the bus and grip the emergency door release bar.

"Open it, Blake," yells Mrs. Greer. "Open it. Hurry!"

And then I hear another voice—one that's not supposed to be here. The voice of Cassandra. She reclines in the back row, calmly watching, amused.

"Hurry, Blake," she mocks. "Not much time left."

"Open it!" screams Mrs. Greer.

But the door is rusted shut. It doesn't budge. "I can't! I can't! I can't!"

"You couldn't open it then," says Cassandra, "and you can't open it now. Such a shame."

Metal scrapes on stone on the belly of the bus. The nose drops lower, the back rises higher, and the bus loses its balance, plunging into Colfax Ravine. I open my mouth to scream, but I am silenced by a blinding, searing explosion, and I am—

★ ★ ★

—*spinning out of control.*

A doomed school bus on an icy day.

Screams, the smell of bubble gum, and Andy Burke falls to the floor.

It's happening all over again! The ride is repeating!

Mrs. Greer wails, "Oh my God, oh my God, oh my God."

No! Not again! I can't go through this again! How many times will it repeat? How many times?

"Hold on, Blake!"

I'm in the aisle again. The smell of rubber and mud. And the emergency exit.

We hit the guardrail and teeter over the edge. I'm at the back now, tugging at the stubborn emergency exit door, and Cassandra is there again, smiling in triumph.

"Here's your own special ride," she tells me. "And you'll never change what happened, no matter how hard you try. You can't change this ride!"

I ram my fist against the emergency exit release until my knuckles are bruised and raw.

"Open it, Blake," screams Mrs. Greer.

"I can't! I can't! I can't!"

We slip off the edge, plunging into the ravine, and the moment before the explosion I can feel Cassandra's breath in my ear as she whispers, "Welcome to eternity."

A blinding flash, and I'm—

—*spinning out of control.*

A school bus on an icy day

Andy falls to the floor.

"Oh my God, oh my God, oh my God."

I've always been on this ride. From the moment that Cassandra, in her bright orange car, cut in front of the bus and sent it spinning out of control, I have been riding. It has dominated my life, playing in my dreams, my daydreams, and every thought I have. This is how Cassandra can trap me— because, in a way, I never left this bus. I've been riding since I was seven years old.

We crash through the guardrail. I drag myself to the back.

If there's a way out of every ride, there has to be a way out of this one. There has to be. What am I not seeing?

You have to remember what you did.

I'm at the emergency exit again as the bus tips at the limit of its balance. My thoughts race too fast to hold on to. If only I could think. There has to be something I'm missing. I survived this accident. How did I do it? I close my eyes. I take a breath.

"Open it, Blake!"

No, Mrs. Greer. No, I won't open it. I have to slow down. I have to think. Force myself to remember. Let *myself remember.*

And all at once a rusty hinge in my head is jarred loose. My eyes snap open.

"This isn't how it happened!"

"What do you mean?" shouts Cassandra. "Of course it's how it happened!"

I turn to her, realizing something for the first time. "You didn't hang around to see, did you? You drove past the bus, cut in front of it, and sent us spinning, but you were gone before we crashed. You never saw what happened!"

"This is your *ride!" she insists. "*Your *memory!"*

"My memory's wrong!"
We slide into the ravine. An explosion, and I'm—

—spinning out of control.
Andy falls.
"Oh my God, oh my God, oh my God."
As real as it seemed before, it's even more real now,
because this time it's not just half the memory—it's the whole
memory.
I fall from my seat, terrified. My face hits the floor.
"Hold on, Blake."
There are other kids in the aisle. Everyone's screaming.
We crash through the rail.
I see the emergency exit door. I'm climbing over my friends
to get out—to get to that back door. Climbing over the backs of
my friends to save myself. I have to get out. I have to. Others
try to climb over me—everyone's in the same panic—but I'm
the fastest. I get there first. The bus tips, and I grab the emer-
gency exit release.
"Open it, Blake!"
I tug and I tug. "I can't, I can't, I—"
And the latch gives. The door opens, swinging wide. I did
open the door! I did! That's what I refused to remember all
those years. I did open that door!
Now I'm standing at the back of the bus. The world
seems to stop, poised on the moment the way the bus is per-
fectly balanced on the edge of the cliff. Balanced. I am the
balance.

★ ★ ★

Suddenly I was no longer on the bus; I was watching the whole scene unfold from the outside. I stood on the icy road, looking up to see my seven-year-old self standing at the open emergency exit door, the bus teetering back and forth, balanced on the edge.

The rear wheels of the bus were high off the ground, so high that from here, I could see the spinning drive-shaft and transmission. The Works.

"Jump, Blake," I heard Mrs. Greer yell from inside the bus. The little boy at the back of the bus—the boy whom I once was—hesitated. It was such a long way down.

As I watched, Cassandra danced around me, thrilled to know the truth of my survival. "You jumped, didn't you! That's why you survived!" Her mud-toned silken shroud fluttered with every motion of her arms. "You jumped out the door, and that's all it took to push the bus over the edge!"

I didn't answer her. I just watched as the little boy at the back of the bus closed his eyes and leaned forward, just as the bus slipped another foot. That terrified little boy somehow found it in himself to leap from the back of the doomed bus. Even though no one else jumped with him. Even though he knew he'd be the only one out. Even with the burden of guilt he would have to bear, he—I—still chose to live. He jumped from the back of the bus, and I opened my arms, catching him. He was almost weightless, his sobs barely audible in my ears as the bus tipped and began its final slide off the edge.

Cassandra stopped her dance and came in so close, I could hear her voice not just as a whisper in my ear, but inside my head. "They all died because you jumped!"

"No," I said calmly. "The bus was going over anyway."

"You'll never know that for sure!"

"No. I won't."

"And you'll never change what happened."

"No. But I can get off this ride. Forever."

The back end of the bus disappeared over the edge. I held the boy in my arms safe from the flash of heat and from the sound of the explosion, knowing this was the last time I'd ever have to hear it. *It's all right, Blake. It's over now. I'll hold you and comfort you, and I'll forgive you for being the lucky one. I forgive you for not being strong enough to hold that bus up with your bare hands and save them all. I forgive you for surviving.* I held him tight, until I realized there was no one at all in my embrace. I was wrapping my arms around myself.

The ride was finally over.

I had made it out.

16

Reality Falling

The world—the real one, that is—takes a lot of abuse, but it just bounces back. Resilient—that's the word. However we try to twist it, whatever weird stuff we throw at it, it still holds firm, always there.

The worlds of Cassandra's park were not so resilient. In the end they turned out to be no more substantial than soap bubbles churned out by The Works. All it took to shut the whole thing down was a well-placed monkey wrench. All it took was one survivor.

As I stood at the icy edge of Colfax Ravine, the mangled guardrail beside me, the heavens and earth began to shake. Cassandra suddenly lost interest in me and looked up with growing dread.

It happened all at once: a sharp tearing of sky and splitting of earth. Gears ejected from the ground. The light of different skies poured into the tearing fabric of the dead gray clouds that covered this scene of my memory.

In the distance the Leaning Tower of Pisa tore a hole in the sky and crashed to the ground. Much closer, a healthy chunk of Mount Rushmore fell from above and took out the road less than a hundred yards away.

As the cracks in the ground widened into fissures, people began to climb out. Freed from The Works, they ran in all directions, delirious with—was it fear or relief? I couldn't tell. Many fell back into the great fissures, unable to escape the park, but many more navigated the hazards to find the falling brick walls and shredding gates that once enclosed the park. I tried to find Maggie and Russ in the crowd, but there were just too many faces.

Did I do this? I had seen Cassandra's Egypt dissolve, but that was only one ride. This was all of them coming undone, collapsing into one another. This was the entire park dying. A gear the size of a manhole cover exploded from the ground, and I ducked to keep from being beheaded. When I looked up again, there was Quinn, spilling from the barren world of black sky and confused road signs onto the cracking asphalt.

The second he saw me, he ran to me, giving me a cool high five and a less-cool hug. "You made it!"

I was too distracted to see Cassandra coming. She hurled Quinn out of her way and slid right up to me. Before I could make a move, I felt her hand on my chest, her nails like talons digging into my skin, growing toward my heart. I was frozen. Paralyzed. Quinn tried to grab her, but the power of her searing, freezing extremes jolted him like an electric surge.

"This isn't over," she hissed. "It can't be over. *I* can't be over."

"Let me go." My voice was so weak, I could barely hear it.

"You'll take me with you." Her other hand was cupped behind my head now, her nails in my scalp.

"No."

"Because of you, I've found fear and have finally experienced loss. Because of me, you've found strength. We've been too much to each other. And so you'll take me with you. I will sleep within you." Her earthen shroud clung to me, dissolving into my flesh, covering me like a cocoon. She pressed closer still. "Your world *needs* me. Needs what I offer, needs what I take." I could feel the cold and the heat of her soul beginning a migration into mine. "There's always room for another theme park. There are always more who want to ride."

She wanted a safe haven within me, lying dormant until she was strong enough to build a new park. I would not be a harbor for a spirit such as this. If my will was my strength, I must make mine stronger than hers.

"No!" I said, much more forcefully than before. I still couldn't move my arms or legs, but there was fear now in her eyes. "There's still one more thing you need to feel. One more experience left." It was difficult, but I raised my arms. I fought to grip her shoulders.

"Experience it with me, Blake."

"No," I told her. "You've got to face this alone." Then I shoved her with the full force of my will. She flew from me as if she weighed nothing at all and landed a dozen yards away on the cracking asphalt.

She pushed herself up, but only enough to look at me,

eyes locking on mine. A shadow grew above her, but she didn't move. Even from a distance, I could feel the extremes of her soul, but I felt them as something more human: fiery, passionate anger joined to a chilling and hopeless longing. But now both extremes were caught in a delicate balance, and she was unable to move as the shadow grew larger all around her.

"Good-bye, Cassandra," I said as a farmhouse plucked from the plains of Kansas came down on her with a deafening crash.

And Cassandra was gone. Not so much as her feet stuck out from beneath the house.

"She was a bad witch," said Quinn.

A strange light glowed around us now, hurting my eyes, making it difficult to see anything.

Quinn looked aside, seeing something that I didn't. "Mom?"

In a flash he was gone, and I felt myself tugged backward into the light. It engulfed me, dissolved me. For a moment I could feel myself stretched apart—my thoughts, my feelings refracting into a rainbow, then refocusing into white light.

The white light of dawn. It shone in my eyes, and I had to squint against it, turning my face away.

I was pressed tightly against a pillow, but it wasn't exactly a pillow. I couldn't move.

"We'll have you out in a second," a voice said beside me. I could hear the tearing of metal, like I did when the park broke down.

A fireman knelt just outside the smashed window of my Volvo. He and a second fireman worked with a massive pair of pliers. The Jaws of Life. I'd seen those things on rescue shows. I tried to shift, but I was pinned by the air bag.

A few yards past the firemen, Maggie talked to a paramedic who was hell-bent on examining her. "I'm all right, really. No, I don't want to sit down, okay?"

"Where is most of the pain?" one of the firemen asked me.

"I don't feel any pain."

The two rescue workers looked at each other ominously, then one went off to prepare the back board they planned to carry me away on. I wiggled my toes to make sure I wasn't paralyzed. Then I fought down the air bag to have a look at what I had hit.

In front of the car was a thick oak tree. I knew that tree. I had almost hit it before we arrived at the park.

"Lucky that tree stopped you, or you might have gone over the edge."

We were in the woods at the edge of the quarry. I'd totaled my car against that tree.

I began to get angrier and angrier as I considered what it all meant. The park was not a hallucination. It wasn't even remotely like a dream. My clothes still smelled of smoke from the dying park . . . but couldn't that be from the smoking wreckage of the car? I could still feel the ache from Cassandra's grip on my chest . . . but couldn't that be from the crash?

No. I refused to accept a car crash as an explanation.

"There was an amusement park," I told the fireman. "There were hundreds of kids . . ."

"I'm sure there were," he said, like I was delusional or something. "You can tell us all about it after we get you out." Well, what did I expect? Did I think he would take my claims seriously? How could he?

That's when the truth hit me, and the truth was so simple, so complete, it was obvious. *Of course* all these things could be rationally explained. It could be no other way. Like I said, reality bends and twists to make room for anything, but in return, the real world demands an explanation for all things. And when there *is* no explanation, it's obliged to create one. Reality merely bent itself a little further than usual to leave me wrapped around this tree. I'm sure if I came home with one of Cassandra's rings clasped in my hand, one of the firemen would just happen to be missing one just like it. Reality prevails at all costs.

The universe was having a little joke on me.

I laughed. The firemen thought I was in pain, and a paramedic arrived, ready to administer triage. "Just another second. Try not to move."

They peeled away the ruined door, and while they hurried to get the back board in place, I stepped out and stood up. They just looked at me, stunned. I suppose people would call it a miracle, walking away from a wreck like this, and I began to wonder if, perhaps, every time someone walked away from a totaled car, they were also subjects of a "reality correction."

Now the paramedic who had been so intent on Maggie came over to me and joined with the others to persuade me that I was gravely injured—no matter how uninjured I felt—and that an observational stint at the hospital was in order. I agreed to undergo whatever mandatory medical attention they required if they would just give me a few minutes to see to my friends.

Maggie stood against a tree, just staring at the wreck, like she couldn't take it in. I went up to her and found myself taking her hand like it was the most natural thing in the world to do.

She looked at me, searching for something. I knew what she needed to hear.

"Yes," I told her. "We were there. It happened."

She relaxed and held my hand tighter. There were a million things we could say to each other. But sometimes, when you get the connection right, those things have even greater value when they're left unsaid.

She looked at my Volvo, which had so valiantly sacrificed its crumple zone for us. "Too bad about your car."

I shrugged. "Who needs a car in New York?"

"So you're really going, then?"

I took her other hand. "I'll fly home every few months. If I don't, Quinn might start thinking he's an only child."

At the mention of Quinn's name she began to tremble. "Quinn . . . is he—"

"Out." I said. Simple as that. No explanation needed.

"Good." She reached into her pocket and handed me her phone. "Call your mom. Just to be sure."

I dialed Mom's cell phone, and she picked up on the first ring.

"Hi, Mom."

"Oh, thank God. I tried the house. No one was home. Where are you?"

"Out with Maggie and Russ. I couldn't sleep."

She went on to tell me how comas are such strange things. One minute you're dead to the world, and the next you're sitting up in a hospital bed playing Scrabble with your future stepfather. Apparently Quinn had woken up a short time ago and immediately asked for ice cream, knowing that kids in hospitals got whatever they wanted.

"The MRI showed a small fatty tumor in his brain," Mom said, her voice trembling. "They say it's benign and totally harmless, but I just don't know, Blake. . . ."

"I'm sure they're right," I said before she could break down in tears. "For all we know, it's been there all his life." If it was, it would go a long way toward explaining his early autism. And a whole lot of other things, for that matter.

"Do you want to talk to him?"

I could hear Quinn in the background trying to convince Carl that *LedZep* was a legitimate Scrabble word. No doubt the *Z* was on a triple letter score, and Quinn wouldn't back down for the world. King Tut still moved for no man.

"That's okay," I said. "Just tell him . . ." I smiled.

"Tell him not to ride the hospital bed up and down too fast. He'll get whiplash."

"Very funny."

I told her that I'd see her at the hospital soon, but I left out the part about how I'd be coming in an ambulance.

There was one more person I needed to see. I found Russ sitting on a boulder, looking out over the quarry. I stood at the edge next to him. I couldn't say cliffs and ledges didn't still bother me, but I could stand at one now and not freak out. There was nothing down in the quarry now, not even morning mist.

"You have to take an ambulance back," I told Russ. "If you're a good boy, they might even let you ride up front."

He nodded, making it clear that he would come when he was good and ready. He wouldn't look at me. I had no idea what to say to him, so I just kicked a stone over the edge. We both waited until we heard it hit bottom.

"Listen, I forgive you, okay?"

He laughed bitterly at that. "Of course you do. You'd even forgive Cassandra if she gave you puppy-dog eyes."

Finally he looked at me. I'm still not sure what I saw in him. Some anger? A hint of the same kind of guilt I had held on to for so many years? Or maybe a lingering memory of the Ferris wheel. He never did tell me what that ride had done to him, and now I suspected he never would. We'd all learned things about ourselves tonight, and I didn't think Russ was too comfortable with what he'd discovered. I could tell he'd been damaged. Not on the outside, but deeper down, where it really mattered. I didn't know if it was the kind of damage he'd ever recover from.

"So. Is there something going on between you and Maggie?" he asked.

"I don't know. Maybe."

He hardened his jaw, looked down at his hand, and clenched his fist until his knuckles were white—although I don't think he knew what he wanted to punch. He held his fist tight for a few seconds, then let it go, shaking out his hand. He returned his gaze to the canyon.

"Don't expect me to write to you at Columbia," he said. But somehow I expect he will.

When I returned to my accordion of a Volvo, two of the paramedics were staring at the smashed front end. I figured they were just marveling at how we could just walk away from a crash like that, but that wasn't it at all.

"Ever see anything like that?" one asked the other.

The other tilted his head to the side and squinted his eyes. As I got closer I could see it too. It was in the crumple pattern of the hood. The way the metal had bent and the way the light hit it, you could swear there was a face in the folds of the metal. Cheekbones, eye sockets, a nose and mouth.

"Optical illusion," said the second paramedic. "A trick of the light, like that face on Mars."

Maybe so. Except that this face was Cassandra's.

I stared into the shadows of her eyes in the crumpled hood, and her gaze held me there for a long time. I didn't know what I was searching for. I didn't know why I couldn't look away. I knew I had to leave because the ambulance was waiting. My life was waiting. But I kept looking at those eyes in the strange wrinkle of steel until a cloud covered the sun, and her face was gone.

Are you dead, Cassandra, or just sleeping? Should I mourn for you or curse you for the things you've done? I suspect she'll always be there, somewhere in the scenery, but I can't let that stop me from living.

"Anything you need from the car?" a fireman asked as a tow truck pulled up.

"No, nothing. Nothing at all."

As I headed toward the ambulance with Maggie and Russ, I thought about tomorrow, and the next day, and the next. I thought about leaving for school, and I felt those familiar butterflies fill my stomach. But they're no longer a source of discomfort.

In fact, I think I kind of like the feeling.

The limbo-land Everlost is at war. On one side stands Mary, self-proclaimed queen of lost souls, determined to retain her iron grip on Everlost's children. On the other is Nick, the Chocolate Ogre, determined to set the souls of Everlost free.

Everlost will never be the same.

Check out the beginning of the second book in the Skinjacker trilogy

CHAPTER 1

Fresh Havoc

There were rumors.

Of terrible things, of wonderful things, of events too immense to keep to oneself, and so they were quietly shared from soul to soul, one Afterlight to another, until every Afterlight in Everlost had heard them.

There was the rumor of a beautiful sky witch, who soared across the heavens in a great silver balloon. And there were whispers of a terrible ogre made entirely of chocolate, who lured unsuspecting souls with that rich promising smell, only to cast them down a bottomless pit from which there was no return.

In a world where memories bleach clean from the fabric of time, rumors become more important than that which is actually known. They are the life's blood of the bloodless world that lies between life and death.

On a day much like any other in Everlost, one boy was about to find out if those rumors were true.

His name is unimportant—so unimportant that he himself had forgotten it—and less important still, because in a brief time he will be gone forever.

He had died about two years earlier, and, having lost his way to the light, he slept for nine months, then had woken up in Everlost. The boy was a wanderer, solitary and silent, hiding from others who crossed his path, for fear of what they might do to him. Without camaraderie and friendship to remind him who he was, he forgot his identity more quickly than most.

On the occasions that he did come across packs of other Afterlight kids, he would listen to them from his hiding spot as they shared with each other the rumors of monsters, so he knew as well as any other Afterlight what lay in store for the unwary.

When the boy had first crossed into Everlost, his wanderings had a purpose. He had begun in search of answers, but now he had even forgotten the questions. All that remained was an urge to keep moving, resting only when he came across a deadspot—a solid, bright patch of earth that had, like him, crossed into Everlost. He had learned very quickly that deadspots were unlike the faded, unfocused world of the living, where every footfall pulled you ankle-deep, and threatened to take you all the way down to the center of the earth if you stood still for too long.

On this day, his wanderings had brought him to a field full of deadspots—he had never seen so many in one place . . . but what really caught his attention was the bucket of popcorn. It just sat there on a deadspot, beside a huge Everlost tree, like it had no better place to be.

Somehow, the popcorn had crossed over!

The dead boy had not had the luxury of food since

arriving in Everlost—and just because he didn't need to eat anymore, it didn't mean the cravings ended—so how could he resist that popcorn? It was the largest size, too—the kind you order with big eyes in the movie theater, but can never finish. Even now the corn inside glistened with butter. It seemed too good to be true!

Turns out, it was.

As he stepped onto the deadspot and reached for the tub, he felt a trip wire against his ankle, and in an instant a net pulled up around him, lifting him off the ground. Only after he was fully snared within the net did he realize his mistake.

He had heard of the monster that called itself the McGill, and his soul traps—but he had also heard that the McGill had traveled far away, and was now wreaking fresh havoc across the Atlantic Ocean. So then, who had set this trap? And why?

He struggled to free himself, but it was no use—his only consolation was that the bucket of popcorn was trapped in the net with him, and although half of its contents had spilled onto the ground, half still remained. He savored every single kernel, and when he was done, he waited, and he waited. Day became night, became day over and over, until he lost track of time, and he began to fear that his eternity would be spent strung up in this net. . . . Until he finally heard a faint droning sound—some sort of engine approaching from the north. The sound was echoed from the south—but then, as both sounds grew louder, he realized it wasn't an echo at all. The sounds were different. He was being approached on two sides.

Were these other Afterlights coming for him, or were they monsters? Would he be freed, or would he become the victim of fresh havoc himself? The faint memory of a heart pounded in his ghostly chest, and as the whine of engines grew louder, he waited to see who would reach him first.

CHAPTER 2

The View on High

M iss Mary, one of our lookouts spotted a trap that's sprung."

"Excellent news! Tell Speedo to bring us down close, but not too close—we don't want to frighten our new friend."

Mary Hightower was in her element this far from the ground. Not so high as the living flew, where even the clouds were so far below, they seemed painted on the earth, but here, in that gap between earth and the heavens, is where she felt at home. She was queen of the *Hindenburg*, and she liked that just fine. The massive silver airship—the largest zeppelin ever built—had gone up in a ball of flames way back in 1937, leaving the living world and crossing into Everlost. Mary, who believed all things happened for a reason, knew why it had exploded: It had crossed into Everlost for her.

The Starboard Promenade, which ran the full length of the passenger compartment, was her plush personal retreat, and her center of operations. Its downward-slanted windows gave her a dramatic view of the ground below: the washed-out hues of the living world, speckled with features both man-made and natural that stood out more boldly than the rest. Those were the places that had crossed into Everlost. Trees and fields, buildings and roads. While Afterlights could still see the living world, it was blurred and faded. Only things and places that had crossed into Everlost appeared bright and in sharp focus. Mary estimated that one in a hundred things that died or were destroyed crossed into Everlost. The universe was very selective in what it chose to keep.

Only now, as she spent her days riding the skies, did she realize she had stayed put for way too long. She had missed so much up in her towers — but then the towers were a citadel against her brother, Mikey — the monster who called himself the McGill. Mikey had been defeated. He was harmless now. And now Mary no longer had to wait for Afterlights to find her. She could go out and find them herself.

"Why are you always looking out of those windows?" Speedo would ask her, when he took a break from piloting the airship. "What do you see?"

"A world of ghosts," she would tell him. Speedo had no idea that the ghosts she spoke of were the so-called living. How insubstantial that world was. Nothing in it lasted, not places, not people. It was a world full of pointless pursuits that always ended the same way. A tunnel, and surrender. *Well, not always*, she thought happily. *Not for everyone.*

"I'd still rather be alive," Speedo would say whenever she spoke of how blessed they were to be here in Everlost.

"If I had lived," Mary would remind him, "I'd be long dead by now . . . and you'd probably be a fat, bald accountant."

Then Speedo would look at his slight physique, dripping wet—always dripping wet in the bathing suit he died in—to reassure himself that he'd never have grown fat and bald, had he lived. But Mary knew better. Adulthood can do the most horrific things to the best of people. Mary much preferred being fifteen forever.

Mary took a moment to gather herself and prepare to greet the new arrival. She would do it personally. It was her way, and it was the least she could do. She would be the first out of the ship—a slender figure in a plush green velvet dress, and with a perfect fall of copper hair, descending the ramp from the impossibly huge hydrogen airship. This is how it was done. With class, with style. The personal touch. All new arrivals would know from the first moment they met her that she loved each and every child in her care and they were safe under her capable protection.

As she left the Starboard Promenade, she passed other children in the common areas of the ship. She had collected forty-seven of them. In her days at the towers, there had been many, many more—but Nick had taken them from her. He had betrayed her, handing each of her children the key to their own undoing. He had placed a coin in each of their hands. The coins! Those horrid little reminders that a true death did await all of them if they were foolish enough to seek it—and just because there was a light at the end of the tunnel, it didn't mean it was something to be desired. Not the way Mary saw it. Heaven might shine bright, but so do flames.

As the ship descended, Mary went to the control car— the ship's bridge which hung from the belly of the giant craft. From there she would have the best view as they descended.

"We should touch down in a few minutes," Speedo told her, as he intently piloted the sleek silver beast. He was one of the few Afterlights to refuse to take a coin on the day Nick betrayed her. That had earned him a special place. A position of trust and responsibility.

"Look at that field." Speedo pointed it out. "Do you see all those deadspots?"

From the air it looked like a hundred random polka dots on the ground.

"There must have been a battle here once," Mary suggested. "Perhaps the Revolutionary War."

There was one Everlost tree, standing on its own deadspot. "The trap is in that tree," Speedo told her as they neared the ground.

It was a grand tree, its leaves full of rich reds and yellows, set apart from the greener summertime trees of the living world. For this tree it would always be the early days of fall, but the leaves would never drop from its branches. Mary wondered what had caused it to cross over. Perhaps lovers had carved their initials in it, and then it was struck by lightning. Perhaps it was planted in someone's memory, but was then cut down. Or maybe it simply soaked up the blood of a fallen soldier, and died years later in a drought. For whatever reason, the tree didn't die entirely. Instead it crossed into Everlost, like so many things that the universe saw fit to preserve.

The foliage of the tree was so dense, they couldn't see the trap, even after they had touched down.

"I'll go first," Mary said. "But I'd like you to come too. I'll need you to free our new friend from the net."

"Of course, Miss Mary." Speedo smiled a smile that was slightly too large for his face.

The ramp was lowered, and Mary stepped from the airship to the earth, keeping the grace of her stride even as her feet sank almost to her ankles in the living world with each step.

But as she got closer to the tree, she saw that something was terribly, terribly wrong. The net had been taken down, and there was no Afterlight inside. All that remained was the empty popcorn tub on the ground—the bait she had left, just as her brother used to—but while the McGill offered his captives slavery, Mary offered them freedom. Or at least her definition of it. But there was no Afterlight in the net to receive her gift today.

"Musta gotten out," Speedo said as he came up behind her.

Mary shook her head. "No one gets out of these nets."

And then a scent came to her from the tree. It was a sweet, heady aroma that filled her with a rich blend of love, swirled with loathing.

The aroma was coming from a brown handprint on the trunk of the tree. A handprint left there to mock her.

"Is that dried blood?" Speedo asked.

"No," she told him, maintaining her poise in spite of the fury that raged within her. "It's chocolate."

PETE
HAUTMAN

SIMON & SCHUSTER | BFYR

TEEN.SimonandSchuster.com